CW01214475

Also by Dillon VanOort

A Heart Full of Light To Bright Up The Night

GOD and Todd

by
Dillon VanOort

FOREVERLAND ENTERTAINMENT PRESENTS
A FOREVERLAND ENTERTAINMENT PRODUCTION "GOD and TODD" A DILLON VANOORT NOVEL
STARRING TODD CARPENTER EMILY CARPENTER IZZY EATON THUNDER SON THE HORSE ERNIE & IRA DOCTOR HEMMING PASTOR NATE
PUBLISHED BY FOREVERLAND ENTERTAINMENT

Foreverland Entertainment
Los Angeles

First Paperback Edition 2024

Published in the United States by Foreverland Entertainment

Copyright © 2024 by Dillon VanOort

All rights reserved. In accordance with the U.S. Copyright Act of 1976, no part of this work may be reproduced or transmitted in any form or by any means, except as may be expressly permitted in writing from the publisher and will constitute unlawful piracy and theft of the author's intellectual property. If you would like to use material from the book, prior written permission must be obtained by contacting the publisher at permissions@foreverlandentertainment.com.

Foreverland Entertainment
Los Angeles, CA

God and Todd is a work of fiction.

The characters, incidents, and dialogue are drawn from the author's imagination and are not to be construed as real. Any resemblance to actual events or persons, living or dead, is entirely coincidental.

Foreverland Entertainment and design are registered trademarks.
The publisher is not responsible for websites and social channels, or their content, that are not owned by the publisher.

Library of Congress Control Number: 2024917489

ISBN: 978-1-7358643-2-7

Printed in the United States of America
10 9 8 7 6 5

For the Big Guy in the sky

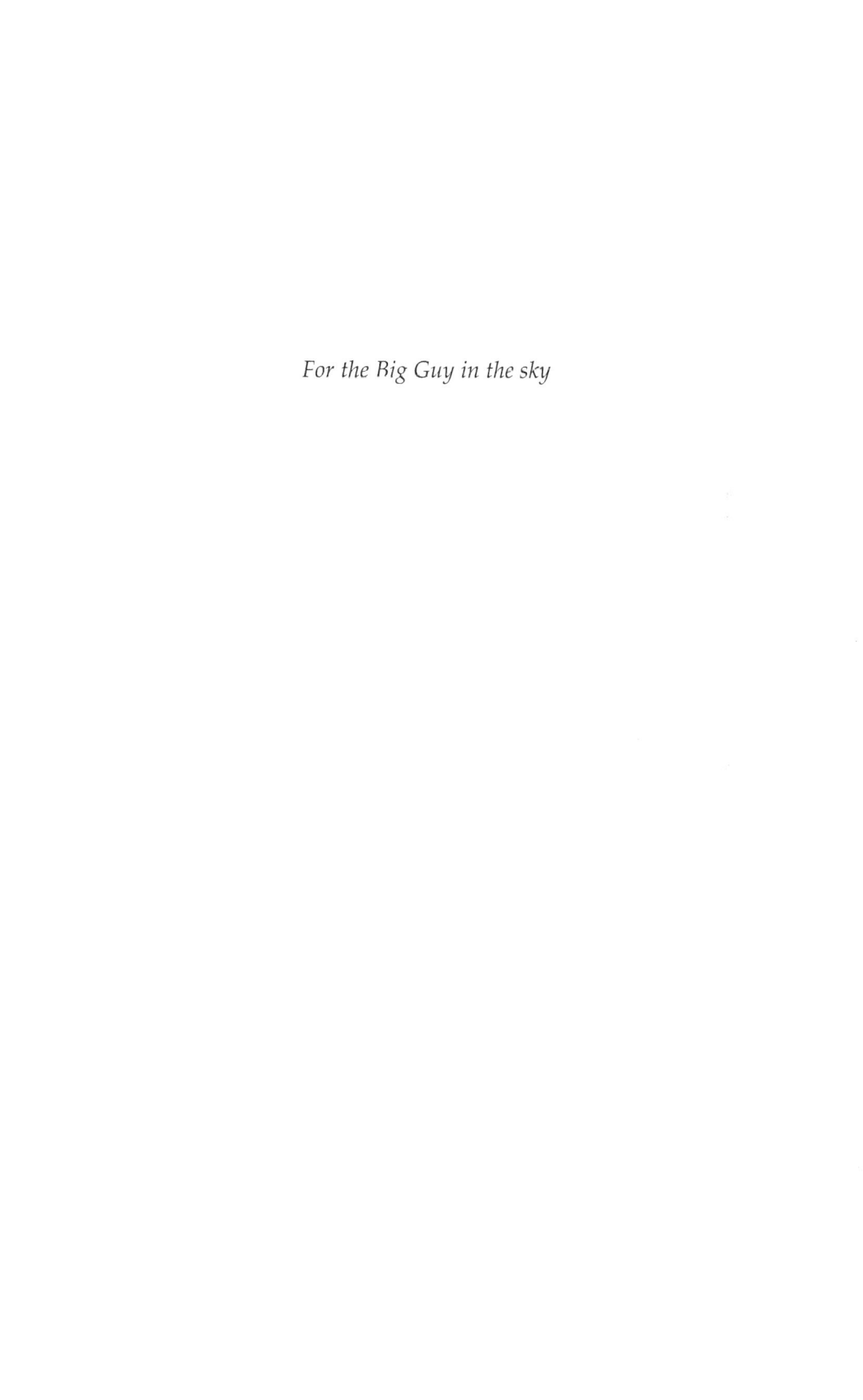

GOD and Todd

One

GOD

God, I died once and came back.

You were watching out for me.

This is a good feeling.

You have been there for me my entire whole life. You are a real truth. I did not always know You were a real truth, but then I did know, and now I do know.

You were a real truth when I did not know You.

You were a real truth when I did know You.

You are a real truth now.

The first time I knew You were a real truth was way back on that day that I got hurt really bad, and they said I died, but I did not die. Because You saved me. They told me that I was lost, but then I was found. They said when I died I would not be any smarter than I am right now, and that I will never be smart ever again. I was seven then. That is the day when I saw Your Bright Light, and that is when I saw the Secret Place, and it was like power hiding in stars, but bigger and that is when You saved me. I heard Your Voice too. And You said, Wake up. So I woke up right then and when I woke up I was in a bed and I was tired. I could not move good or see good or talk good or think good and I still cannot do any of these good. They said I was sleeping for five entire whole months and I did not move once in that entire whole time. But then I woke up, and I remember this because Emily was sitting in a chair next to my bed waiting for me and mom was too. But mom is dead now, she has been dead for a while.

Some say I am dumb to believe in You.

I am dumb and I know that is a truth.

But You are real and that is also a truth.

That is why I believe in You. I believe in You because You are the True God, and that is the biggest truth there ever was. I believe in You because You are the God of the Bible, which means there are no other Gods either. I believe in You because You raised Jesus Christ from the dead because He is Your Son, and also You raised me too because I was dead, but now I am not. That is a truth.

I believe in You because the day I got hurt real bad, I went to church for the first time ever, and that is when I asked Jesus to be the Master of my life and You saved me. That was back when I was Body Seven. Pastor Nate scared us that Sunday and said when you die you either go to Heaven or hell, and you choose, and once you die, there are no take backs. He said the only way to Heaven is to trust Jesus Christ to save you because He is the only Son of God who died for your sins and only He can. Then you ask Him to be Master of your life and do what He says the best you can, because He has fun plans for your life, and it is the best plan. Then Pastor Nate said if anyone wanted to give their life to Jesus, now is the time because tomorrow might not be here. I did not know where tomorrow was going, but I did not want to miss it. So I stood up and everyone was quiet, and they watched me walk to the front of the church all alone.

Pastor Nate said, Kid, do you understand what you are doing?

I said, Avoiding eternal damnation, sir.

Pastor Nate laughed, and so did the rest of the people, but I did not, because it was not funny, it was serious. Then we prayed, and I said I was sorry for my sins, and I asked for Jesus to save me, and He did, and I knew it was a truth. Then Pastor Nate said that I was lost and now I am found. Then Pastor Nate looked at me and told me that I just got saved.

Later that day is when I got hurt really bad and they said I died. This was a bad feeling. But God, You saved me, and I came back.

This is a good feeling.

Two

TODD

My name is Todd.

I am thirty-three years old.

But I am also seven.

Doctor Hemming says I will have the brain of a seven-year-old for the rest of my life, and he says I have had the brain of a seven-year-old ever since I was a seven-year-old and that is why I am seven. This makes it weird when people talk to me sometimes because I look like I am lots older, but I am not. When I look at myself all I see is a seven-year-old, because that is who I am. And sometimes people ask me how old I am, and I say I am thirty-three, but I say also I am a seven-year-old. People think this is weird, and I guess it is.

I do not think You think this is weird.

I think You already know this.

Because You are God.

Pastor Nate says I should tell You this anyway so I can know You and so You can know me, but you already know me. He also said I have to spell things right and to put the commas and periods and stuff in all the right places. I am trying to spell right and I am trying to put the commas and periods and stuff in all the right places, but I do not know when it is right to use commas and periods and stuff so I will use them when I feel like it. Also, Pastor Nate tried to teach me about sentences and paragraphs and when they start and when they end, but it is something I did not understand, and it is something I still do not understand.

A sentence should begin when I begin it, and it should end when I end it. This is the best way. Pastor Nate said this is wrong, and I like Pastor Nate, but he is not God. You are God. I think You want me to be me. So that is what I am going to do and how I am going to write. I am going to talk to You this way. Sometimes I talk to You in my head, because that is praying too. Sometimes I talk to You out loud, but Pastor Nate said only do that when I am alone or else it is weird. He said if people are around I should only talk to You in my head thinking good thoughts. This is hard to do because I do not think right. If I cannot think right then I cannot pray right. Also sometimes there are other voices in my mind that talk and they are scary to me. They are bad. They say bad things, and I do not know if the voices are mine or someone else. That is why it is so scary. So Pastor Nate told me to write to You, and that is what I am doing, so I will start again.

My name is Todd.

I am thirty-three years old.

But I am also seven.

My favorite things are comic books and movies and superheroes and Star Wars and King Arthur and I like reading lots of stories and I like writing lots of stories and I like watching movies and I like listening to Bruce Springsteen and also sneakers are cool and horses too. I wish I had a horse. If I had one I would name it Thunder Son. But I do not, so I have these other favorite things. Some of these things I can still do and some of these things I cannot do anymore.

But I still like all these things.

A long time ago I was smart, and my mom told me I was. This is a truth. This is when I was Body Seven. And one time my mom found out I was smart and she stared at me for a long time and did not talk. I remember because I just do. This day was after school, and my mom was watching a cooking show and making cookies because she liked to make cookies and I liked to eat them. I brought her my math homework, and told her I was done, and it was easy.

She said, Great, now do Emily's math homework because she's failing.

So I went to find Emily's math homework, and I did it. And I also did her math homework fast and brought it to my mom. I said, Mom, look, I did her math homework fast, and it was easy, and also everything is right and a truth.

My mom was still cooking and watching television and not looking at me. She said, Yes, sweetie. Maybe you can do Emily's physics homework now.

So then I went upstairs and found a book called Physics, and did that too, and it was easy. I brought it to my mom and she was still cooking and watching television and she was not looking at me. I said, Mom, look, I did Emily's Physics, it was easy and everything is right and a truth.

She said, Do me a favor while you're on a roll and go read that book that Emily's gotta read for English because we all know she won't do that either.

So I went upstairs and found a book in her bag called The Catcher In The Rye by a person named J.D. Salinger, and I read it and it was easy. I went back downstairs to my mom and she was still cooking and still watching television and she was still not looking at me.

I said, Mom, I did Emily's math homework and her physics homework and I read the book she has to read for English called The Catcher In The Rye by a person named J.D. Salinger.

She said, It's been five minutes, sweetie, and it's not nice to lie.

I said, Mom, I did all these things and that is a truth.

Then I proved it, because sometimes you have to prove a truth, because sometimes people do not believe truths, because sometimes people need proof of a truth, or sometimes they do not like the truth that you have proved to them so they do not believe that what you said is a truth. So I proved it. I showed my mom the math homework, and the physics homework, and the book I read called The Catcher In The Rye by a person named J.D. Salinger. She looked at me, then she looked at the books, then she looked at me again. This time she did not say anything. This is when my mom knew I was smart.

She told lots of people on the phone.

I know because I heard her on the phone.

But I read my comic books and did not care.

Then it was a few days later, and Doctor Hemming came up to me after school while I waited for the school bus to go home, and he asked what I wanted to be when I grew up. Doctor Hemming was with my teacher, and with some other scientist people and my mom was there too. I remember this because I just do.

The day was over so I was leaving school. So I did not want to answer, I wanted to go home, so I said I did not know. Then Doctor Hemming asked if I would like to take some tests to figure out what I wanted to be when I grew up. I said no because all the other kids were going home and I wanted to go home too. And also, I did not care what I was going to be when I grew up because I was seven then and I still am. But they made me take the tests and I had to take them until it was dark. I did not deserve this because I did not do anything bad. I said this, but they did not care. They said it was serious. So I took the tests and they were easy, but I do not remember the tests anymore.

Then it was a few days later.

And they made me stay after school again.

But this time they gave me pizza.

This time, Doctor Hemming and my teacher and the scientist people and my mom were happy because they said I scored perfect. Doctor Hemming said I was a smart boy and maybe even one of the smartest in the entire whole world. Then Doctor Hemming said to tell him and my teacher and the scientist people and my mom about some things that I like. So I told him my favorite things are comic books and movies and superheroes and Star Wars and King Arthur and I also like reading lots of stories and I like writing lots of stories and also I like watching lots of movies and I like listening to Bruce Springsteen and also sneakers are cool and horses too, and I wish I had a horse and if I did I would name it Thunder Son. Then they laughed but I did not understand why because everything I said was a truth. Then they stopped laughing and Doctor Hemming asked what I wanted to be when I grew up. I still did not know because I was seven then and I still am. But I said I wanted to make people happy with stories.

Stories are fun.

They make people think.

Stories make people feel.

A truth is I liked to write stories. When I was Body Seven I used to write stories about space battles and adventures in my town, which is called Morning, New York. Sometimes I wrote poems. What I really liked to write the most was Mini Movies. I wrote many Mini Movies. They were fun. They were about heroes and big and fun and cool adventures. Sometimes I try to write now but then it is hard to think. So I do not write anymore except this, which I am writing now, and this is hard too. I also used to read books. When I was smart, I read a book once called The Once and Future King by a person named T.H. White. I liked it. When I was smart I also read Peter Pan by a person named J.M. Barrie and I liked that too. So I read both books one hundred and ten times in one day because that is when I could read fast and remember everything and I decided they were my favorite books. It is hard to read and remember books now. I do not read now. Except the Bible. The Bible is the only book I can read and remember. I do not know why, but it is a truth. I think You give me power to remember. This makes me happy. Other books are hard to read and even harder to remember. Sometimes when I try to read books, the words do not look like words, they look like other things I do not understand. It is like when I look in the mirror. I do not understand. When I look at myself in the mirror I do not see the me that other people see. I see me as I am, a seven-year-old, and this is a truth, but I am also thirty-three, and this is a truth too. Sometimes a truth is sad because it makes you know things you do not want to know.

    One truth I remember is after I took the tests. My mom said she was proud of me and said I could be anything I wanted in the entire whole world. Then she took me for ice cream. She cried when we ate our ice cream. I asked her why she was crying because I did not understand because ice cream is always a happy thing. I did not like her sad. She said she was happy. I had never seen someone who was happy and crying before in my life. She said I was a prodigy. She asked if I knew what prodigy meant, and I knew, but I did not say anything to my mom right then. I wanted to say that a prodigy is like in X-Men when Professor X uses his mutant powers and Cerebro to make himself smarter and more powerful except I did not need Cerebro or mutant powers and that is because I could be smart all by myself. But I did not say this to my mom because she would not understand and she wanted to tell me so I let her tell me. She said a prodigy meant I was smart. She said I was a smart boy, and maybe one of the smartest boys in the entire whole world. This was a truth. I used to be smart.

    This was a good feeling.

Three

MY
BEST
FRIEND

God, You are my best friend.

Now I am going to tell you why.

It is because You understand me.

Nobody understands me. Sometimes I do not understand myself either. That is my fault. It is because when I say words, people do not hear what I mean, and sometimes I say only wrong words. That is why I have not many friends and no best friends, because nobody understands what I say to them. So I do not talk to people much, because I learned they do not hear me. I say only things they know. I do not try to make people understand me because they will not understand and then be sad. But God, You understand me. I talk to You all the time. The best is when I talk to You with my mouth. That way I know what I am saying. I do not like talking with just my mind because it is too hard to do. Sometimes when I talk with only my mind I say things I do not want to say to You and would never say. That is because there other voices in my mind and they say bad things I would never say. When I talk with my mind I get confused about what I have said and what I did not say to You. When I talk with my mouth I know what I have said because I have said it and then I know. But sometimes, I cannot say what I want to say with my mouth because I do not know all the words.

Sometimes I forget what I want to say.

And sometimes I do not know what to say.

Sometimes I say things that make people mad.

When I was Body Eight, Emily and me went to the store and I wanted to say something to her. Emily was driving and I was in the car with her and we got to the bridge where I died. I had a hurt and wanted to say something, but I did not know what to say. So all I said was No.

She said, What?

I said, No.

And I said it loud. Then I said No again.

She said, Stop being a spaz.

I said, No.

But this time I said it even louder. I did not know what else to say and she did not understand. Emily kept driving and told me to calm down. Then I said, No, and I said it a whole lot of times in a row. I did not know why. Then Emily drove across the bridge and I cried loud and she did not like it at all. She asked what was wrong, but I did not know. I cried all the way to the store and I could not stop. When we got to the store Emily said I could not go in because I was crying too much. I said no again. Then I opened the door and ran away from the car in the parking lot and Emily had to chase me all over. But Pastor Nate caught me because he was also in the parking lot right then and he hugged me. He asked me many questions and I told him the answers. He asked me why I said no to Emily. The answer was because I saw the bridge where I died. Then Pastor Nate said that he understood me. That is because You made him understand. If it were not for You then Pastor Nate would not ever understand. He told me this is why I cried. I just forgot what I was writing. I do not know what I wanted to say.

I forget a lot.

Sometimes You remind me. Other times I remind myself. That is why I get help from Doctor Hemming. He helped me make my calendar called The Calendar of Todd. Before I made The Calendar of Todd, I could not remember almost anything. Now when things happen and they are important, I write it down. Now I can remember lots and lots of things.

I remember what I want to say right now.

What I want to say is this.

You understand me, God.

You understand me because You are God. You are also my Dad. Dads can understand their sons. I had a Dad, but he is in Heaven with You now. So I have not had a Dad for a long time. Dads understand their sons, and they are supposed to be with their sons. I do not have a Dad in this life, but I do have You. This makes a truth to me. Because nobody can be with me except You anyway. That is because only You can do anything. You are the Ruler of the Universe. That is a big deal. Because You are Ruler of the Universe I make sure to capitalize Your Name. I think this is right. And because You are Ruler of the Universe, You can be with everyone everywhere all of the time no matter what. That is why You are with me now. I think about this and it is a cool thing. Sometimes people are there for me, but You are with me. I know this because You said it in the Bible. The Bible says, Greater is he who is in you than he who is in the world. And this is from I John 4:4. I know what this means, God. This means You are in my soul and You are way stronger and better than the one in the world. The one in the world is the devil. He is a liar and he sucks. I should not say suck, but it is a truth. That is why You sent Jesus Christ to save us. Pastor Nate says Jesus is called the Son of God because it is what You are called as a human, even though You are still God. Jesus is You. You are Jesus. But You are also You. You are also the Holy Spirit. This is called the Holy Trinity. This is something I do not understand, but also I do understand. I do not know this in my head, but I know this in my heart. I know this because You let me know this. That is because You always understand me. I wanted to understand the Holy Trinity once but I did not know how to say it but You knew I wanted this so You let me understand because You are my Dad.

Sometimes I understand You.

But You always understand me.

This is because You are my Dad.

You are my best friend too. Having a friend is okay, but having a best friend is better because best friends do not leave. You have not ever left me. This is why You are my best friend. And this is a truth.

But I know another truth.

I do not deserve Your Friendship.

Because I am a bad person.

I did a bad thing. I think this is why I got dumb. But I do not know. Because after I did the bad thing is when I got hurt and died. And I deserved to die too. When people do bad things like I did a bad thing, they deserve to die. That is what happened to me. I died. But You are not mad at me. That is a truth. I know this because You let me see You in the Secret Place. I was small and You were bigger than the whole Universe and You held my hand and we walked together. We walked across the Universe and You showed me many things I do not remember, but it was good. It was fun and I want to do it again. You said You forgave me and that everything was going to be okay. And I know that is a truth. But then sometimes I do not know even though I do know. I am sorry for that. Right now I know that You forgive me and that everything is okay. This is why I am happy now. Because we are best friends. You have never ever left me and I know You will never leave me either. Best friends never leave each other no matter what. But sometimes best friends argue and get mad. Also sometimes best friends do not talk to each other for a little while and that is not good either. But best friends are always best friends. It is like Calvin and Hobbes. They are best friends always. They play together and Calvin always tells Hobbes his problems and Hobbes is always there for him. Except that Hobbes is an imaginary tiger and You are not. You are the Ultimate Supreme Being who made all things. That means You are like my Dad, but also more. You are my best friend, but also more. That gives me a bunch of hope. Because I am not a good person.

But You are still my best friend.

So You always have to be with me.

That is a truth.

Four

MINI MOVIES

I have some favorite things.
And some favorite favorite things.
But then I have the most favorite things.
My most favorite thing is Mini Movies. Mini Movies are like previews before a movie. Previews are also called trailers. I do not know why I call them Mini Movies. Mini Movies are fun. I watch them and when I like one I tell Emily I want to see the Big Movie because the Mini Movie was good. When I was Body Seven and smart I learned how to write Mini Movies. I wrote them in a special way. I do not know how to do it now, but I did then because I was smart. At first I called them Screenplay Mini Movies, but then I just called them Mini Movies. Some were about space and some were about King Arthur and some were funny and some were sad and some were about other things I do not remember. I found them in my closet from many years ago when I was smart. It is hard to read now so I do not read them, but I remember them. I remember they were like dreams but more than dreams. Some of them felt like the future and like they were going to happen. But I do not remember more. It is like a dream in your head when you wake up but then you do not remember the dream. You only remember you had a dream that you forgot. That is how it is with the Mini Movies.
They are dreams you forget.
Maybe it is better to forget dreams that cannot be.
I think that is why they are my most favorite.

PRESENTING A MINI MOVIE EPISODE OF
THE ADVENTURES OF TODD

IN

TODD
and
THUNDER SON THE STARFIGHTER: THE BATTLE TO SAVE THE UNIVERSE

A Science Fiction EPIC
Part I
A Mini Movie by Todd

written for the screen by Todd Carpenter on Saturday, November 9th, 1996

OVER BLACK.

Analog film texture flickers the screen at twenty-four frames per second, the changeover dot winks in the far upper right corner to signify the hallmark of a movie trailer, and with the crackling from the sound comes --

Trailer Voice.

>					NARRATOR (V.O.)
>				From the far reaches of space,
>				deep beyond our own galaxy comes a
>				menace headed for our world.

SPACE.

A void of black scattered with stars and sailing through that endless darkness comes --

ONE UGLY ALIEN MOTHERSHIP.

The monstrosity looks like a fanged alligator mouth of actual teeth built from some bizarre amalgam of advanced circuitry and organic material with electric power coiling the ship.

>					NARRATOR (V.O.)
>				An evil alien armada with a ship so
>				ugly it actually chews up planets.

The alien ship flies toward a bright blue radiant world, its mouth opening wider than the world itself and --

CRUNCH --

The mouth snaps shut, eating the planet. It opens its mouth and spits out a hunk of rock, mangled and dead.

>					NARRATOR (V.O.)
>				There is only one in the universe who
>				can save us from this horror.

TODD.

Seven years old, sitting cross-legged on a grassy hill, late in the evening, staring up at the stars.

>					NARRATOR (V.O.)
>				A young boy watching the night sky.

By his side --

A WHITE HORSE, oddly, lays down beside Todd. The boy pets the horse as he keeps his eyes on the sky.

> NARRATOR (V.O.)
> A young boy who dreams of traveling the cosmos --

Todd makes a hole with his thumb and index finger, circling the moon. He gazes through the hole at the moon where a speck illuminates into --

A small flash.

Todd lowers his hand.

> NARRATOR (V.O.)
> Who dreams of becoming a hero --

He focuses in on the area in the sky and -- another flash where the moon floats -- and another even brighter flash blinks again to reveal an object of some kind.

> NARRATOR (V.O.)
> Who dreams of **adventure.**

A bright sphere. It speeds up. Coming closer, closer. The sphere appears to be headed toward Todd. The boy jumps up and gets on the horse as the sphere travels closer, increasing in size and speed, gaining, gaining, gaining, faster, faster, **faster** --

FOOM --

The thing crashes into the bottom of the grassy hill, kicking up dirt and debris and a smoke plumb, while Todd and his horse ride toward it --

TODD.

On his horse as it trots, covered in soot. Todd coughs and waves the dust away. He approaches the newly formed dust cloud, where within -- **A GLOWING SPHERE** blinking **ON** and **OFF** and speaking in a soothing but robotic tone.

> ALIEN SPHERE
> Greetings, human. I am an alien, one of the good ones, I promise, and I am here to warn you the bad aliens are coming to your world. I have traveled a great distance to find a hero. You are that hero. You have been chosen as champion.

                    TODD
          Champion? To do what?

                    ALIEN SPHERE
          To save the universe of course.

                    TODD
          Cool.

THE ALIEN SPHERE.

TRANSFORMS into a ship. It sprouts wings, a fuselage, a cockpit, gun turrets and missile launchers, turning into a fighter jet of some kind, more advanced than the world has ever seen, sleek and black and space ready.

A living starfighter.

Todd dismounts his horse.

                    ALIEN STARFIGHTER
          Come, join me, and we will fight
          the bad aliens together.

                    TODD
          What about my horse?

                    ALIEN STARFIGHTER
          I am your horse. I downloaded the
          mind of this being who is close to
          you in order to understand you
          better. Your horse is me, I am it.
          What will you name me?

Thunder in the sky -- it catches Todd's attention.

                    TODD
          I will call you -- **Thunder Son.**

TODD.

Now inside the cockpit, buckling the harness straps and holding tight to the steering yoke. The canopy lowers and seals him inside the starfighter.

                    NARRATOR (V.O.)
          Now with his new friend, one of the
          good aliens who is also a starfighter
          and somehow contains the mind of
          Todd's horse named Thunder Son,
          our hero travels to the far side of
          the universe.

Thunder Son, the living alien starfighter with the additional
consciousness of a horse, points upward toward the sky --

                    THUNDER SON THE STARFIGHTER
          Initiating faster than light travel.

                          TODD
          Faster than what?

BLAST OFF.

Todd jolts back in his seat from the gravitational force,
the steering yoke shakes, Todd shakes, the craft shakes and
lights zoom all over in this faster-than-light travel.

THUNDER SON THE STARFIGHTER.

Now in space zooming near a nebula. Inside the craft,
Todd stares out the canopy window in awe.

                      NARRATOR (V.O.)
          He will encounter wonder.

ASTEROIDS.

Hundreds head for the lone starfighter -- Thunder Son the
Starfighter dodges with barrel rolls and firing lasers --

                    NARRATOR (V.O.)
          He will encounter danger.

TODD.

He grips the steering yoke and turns it, dodging asteroids --

                                          CUT TO:

THE UGLY ALIEN MOTHERSHIP

In deep space, launching its own spherical starfighters that
look like spiky basketballs, hundreds of them out the fanged
mouth of this really ugly thing, heading for --

Thunder Son the Starfighter --

TODD.

In the cockpit of Thunder Son, flicking controls on the dash.

                    TODD
          They've launched spherical
          starfighters that look like spiky
          basketballs. What do we do?

                    THUNDER SON THE STARFIGHTER
          We must attack to save the
          universe.

                    NARRATOR (V.O.)
          And he will encounter courage.

                    TODD
          Then attack we must.

SPACE.

The fanged alien starship and Thunder Son the Starfighter face off against evil spiky basketball ships firing lasers while Thunder Son returns fire, blowing up bad guy ships --

                    NARRATOR (V.O.)
          Starring --

THUNDER SON THE STARFIGHTER.

Flashing lights on its wings and maneuvering in space amongst lasers firing omnidirectional --

                    NARRATOR (V.O.)
          Thunder Son, the good guy alien who
          is a living starfighter with the
          mind of a horse but also more --

THE UGLY ALIEN MOTHERSHIP

Firing lightning bolt red lasers at Todd's ship, blowing up some of its own spiky basketball fighters in the process --

                    NARRATOR (V.O.)
          The bad guy aliens with a ship that
          looks like an alligator mouth --

TODD.

Inside the cockpit, turning the steering yoke right, left, up, down, and firing missiles and lasers while screaming in murderous rage against the evil aliens --

                    NARRATOR (V.O.)
          And Todd, the hero, in the most
          epic science fiction saga you will
          ever see in **your entire life** --

SPACE.

Again the void of black scattered with stars while a title
overlays the screen --

                    NARRATOR (V.O.)
          **Todd and Thunder Son the
          Starfighter: The Battle to Save the
          Universe. Part One.** Coming to a
          star system near you this summer.
          Rated PG Thirteen.

                                        CUT TO BLACK.

TODD
AND
THUNDER SON THE STARFIGHTER: THE BATTLE TO SAVE THE UNIVERSE

FOREVERLAND ENTERTAINMENT presents
A FOREVERLAND ENTERTAINMENT production "TODD AND THUNDER SON THE STARFIGHTER: THE BATTLE TO SAVE THE UNIVERSE: PART I"
A TODD CARPENTER mini movie
starring TODD CARPENTER THUNDER SON aka THE HORSE aka ALIEN STARFIGHTER aka GLOWING ALIEN SPHERE aka GOOD GUY ALIEN
BAD GUY ALIENS BAD GUY ALIEN STARSHIP WITH A FANGED MOUTH SPIKY BASKETBALL BAD GUY ALIEN SHIPS
design by TODD
distributed by FOREVERLAND ENTERTAINMENT

Five

THE CHRONICLES OF EMILY PART I

My sister is Emily.

She is forty-five.

I wish she would run away.

Emily has taken care of me almost my entire whole life and she says she will take care of me for the rest of my entire whole life. Sometimes people think Emily is my mom because she takes care of me. She hates this because she says she looks twenty-nine. But when Emily was twenty-nine, people said she was my mom and she did not like it then either. Emily takes care of other people too. She is a nurse. She does not like it because she says she has to listen to doctors complain, and nurses complain, and sick people complain, and she holds hands with sick people when they die sometimes. I want someone to hold my hand when I die. But I do not want Emily to hold my hand when I die because I do not want her to be sad. I want Emily to go away and never come back because that is what she wants. But she will not do this. Emily will take care of me until I die.

But Emily does not want to take care of me.

She does not want to be a nurse either.

Those things make her sad.

Her favorite things are Christmas movies, comic books, cartoons, drawing and she likes listening to Prince and also she thinks sneakers are cool too. Some of these things she does when people are around and some of these things she does when nobody is around.

Emily likes to draw.

But she pretends not to like it.

That is because drawing makes her sad.

Emily is a good drawerer. When I was Body Seven and smart, Emily said she wanted to be a drawerer and make drawings for the rest of her entire whole life. This is a truth. This is when I was Body Seven. Now I am Mind Seven and Body Thirty-Three. When I was Body Seven, me and Emily made a comic book called The Adventures of Emily and Todd. It was Emily and me having lots of adventures. I wrote the stories and Emily drew the pictures. In our stories we went into space sometimes, and sometimes we were on other planets, and sometimes we were in the oceans, and sometimes we were in the jungle, and sometimes we were in the desert and sometimes we were flying with the birds because Emily would draw us wings so we could fly with the birds. When I was smart, Emily drew a picture of me being real smart. I cannot find it anymore. But I remember it because I just do. It was me as Body Seven fixing a machine and there was a nice note that said To The Coolest and Smartest Boy in the Entire Whole World. I have never forgotten that note. It made me real happy. Emily always draws things that make people happy. Some people draw scary or bad things. Emily does not do that. She draws nice and good things. She is a good drawerer. I think she is the best drawerer. I wish I could draw like Emily.

Emily can draw anything.

She is drawing a new comic book.

It is a long comic book about her life.

This new comic book that Emily is drawing is called The Chronicles of Emily Carpenter. She has many drawings in this book. I should not know about her book, and Emily does not know that I know about her book, but I do know. It is how I know many things about Emily that she does not want me to ever know. I know this is wrong because it is private property, but I wanted to look at the nice drawings. But that is also not the Truth Reason I wanted to look at her book. God, I cannot lie to You. The Truth Reason I wanted to look at her book is because I want to know more about Emily. This is because Emily does not tell me things like before when I was smart, and that is because I am no longer smart.

When I was smart, Emily said I was beyond my years and I do not know what that means but she said many things to me like that back when I was smart. When I got dumb, Emily did not talk to me anymore because I cannot understand her life. But I want to understand her. That is because I love her. So I want to know more about her. That is the Truth Reason why I read her new book.

Her book has many parts.

But I have only read Part One.

I have read Part One ten times.

Part One has many things about Emily. It also has many drawings and it was easy to read. That is because there are many drawings in it. Reading is hard, but it is easy when there are drawings. There is also Part Two and Part Three and Part Four and Part Five and more Parts after that. I did not read the other parts. I did not read them because they are long. But that is not an entire whole truth. It is only a part truth. I have not read the other parts because I am afraid to read the other parts because Part One was sad. Part One has many things I did not know about Emily that I did not want to know, but now I do know.

Some things I have forgotten.

Other things I remember.

Many things I wish I did not know.

One thing I know is the time when I was Body Seven and Emily ran away. But nobody knows about that time. I do not remember she ran away because I did not see it. But I know this because it is in her book. Some things about this I remember because I was there and some things about this I do not remember because I was not there. I remember because I was there for some of it, but I was not there for all of it. It happened at night. I was in the living room alone. And I wanted to watch Star Wars but I did not know how to watch it. That is because this was right after I got not smart and there were many things that I could not do. I asked my mom if I could watch Star Wars and she said yes. So I went to the living room to watch it. When I was in the living room I held the tape but I did not know how to make it go inside the television. Then I went back to my mom and asked her to make it work, but she was sleepy and sad in bed and she told me to ask Emily. So I went to find Emily, but I could not find Emily because Emily was not home. So I went into the kitchen and Emily was not there. I went to her room and Emily was not there. I went to the backyard and Emily was not there. I went to the bathroom but Emily was not there. So I went to the driveway and that is where I found Emily. She wore a yellow raincoat and she was wearing big sunglasses even though it was dark and she was chewing bubble gum. I remember this because she looked like Jubilee from X-Men. She had two big bags on the ground next to her with her backpack on and a book in her hand.

I said, I want to watch Star Wars and do not know how to make it work.

This made her cry.

So I said, Emily, why are you crying?

She hugged me.

She said, Just remember that I was a very very dumb nineteen-year-old girl who couldn't handle it, okay?

I said, I do not know what that means, Emily.

She laughed. But she cried too. Then I saw car headlights. A car came to our driveway. Emily picked up her bags and put them in the car. There was a boy driving the car who I did not know, but then did I know him later and his name was Jacob, but I did not like him back then or later either because he is bad and sucks. Emily kissed me on the cheek and did not say anything. She just cried lots and lots and got into the car with Jacob who sucks. The car drove away and I did not know where to go so I stayed there. I cried. I cried because Emily was gone. I did not want to ask my mom because my mom would not do anything except be sleepy and sad in bed. That is why I stayed in the driveway. But I still did not know where to go so I stayed there and I cried. And when I was crying I was saying to You, God, please make Emily come back because I miss her lots.

I cried for a long time.

It started raining.

I cried in the rain.

Then I saw lights from a car and the car was driving to our driveway and I knew it was Emily. I knew it was Emily because in my heart I asked God to make her come back. That is how I knew she would come back. Emily got out of the car with her bags and she was crying too. Emily gave me a big hug and held my hand and asked if I was hungry and I said yes. She asked if I wanted mac and cheese, and I said yes to that too. I gave her my Star Wars tape and she said she would put it on for me. It is what I remember. But the things I do not remember I do not remember because I did not see it. And I only know all these things because Emily wrote all these things. She wrote this in The Chronicles of Emily Carpenter Part One. There are the other things that I saw in her book too. I saw in her book she drew pictures of her packing her bags. She drew pictures and wrote words that said she wanted to move to New York City. She said she did not like New York City, but Jacob wanted to go and she said she would go too. She said she was going to draw comic books all day and be happy. She was not happy because of me. That is because she said she had to take care of me all the time because my mom was sleepy and sad in bed all the time and because I was smart but then got dumb. This was in her book. And in the pictures and the words of the book, Emily got in the car with Jacob and wanted to go, but she did not go. She came back. She said God told her to go back home, and I know this because I prayed so I thank You, God. She ran away, but she came back.

    Emily will always take care of me.

    But she does not want to.

    She wants to be a drawerer.

    I know all this because I read The Chronicles of Emily Carpenter Part One. Emily says many things in Part One. There are more parts. She also said she wants to move to Montana and live on a ranch where she can be alone and happy. That is where she can draw all the time and things will be quiet. That is what Emily said in her book. That is a truth. One truth is that Emily did not want to take care of me because she did not want to, but then she did and now she does. Another truth is that Emily still loves me, but Emily also hates taking care of me. She wants to run away again but she wrote she will never run away again.

    I just wish she would.

Six
A Picture for Doctor Hemming

God, You have made all people.

You have made Doctor Hemming.

He is my friend.

Doctor Hemming is an unbeliever. That means he does not trust in You, God. I do not know why the word is called unbeliever, I think the word should be called an untruster. That is because believing in God really means trusting in God, but people say believe. Doctor Hemming does not believe in God, so this means he does not trust in God, so he is an untruster. I do not like this. I also do not like his mustache, but Emily does like his mustache and says it is manly. This makes me feel weird. But this does not matter. What I do not like most is that he is an untruster. That is because if a person does not trust in God, that person does not have hope in their heart. Some people say they believe in God, but they still have no hope because they do not really believe in God and that means they do not really trust in God and so when they say they believe in God, they are lying. A truth is when a person says they believe in God and they trust in God, so they trust Jesus Christ and do what He says. It is an easy thing to trust in God and do what Jesus Christ says because it is always good and a truth. If a person has no hope in God, they have no hope at all. They do not have hope for this life or the next life, and that is really bad. It is bad because if a person has no hope for this life or the next, then they are probably not going to Heaven. They are going somewhere else. It makes me sad because it is a bad thing and it does not have to be that way. All they have to do is believe that You raised Jesus Christ from the dead and ask for forgiveness for their sins then believe that God forgives them and also do what You say. This is not a hard thing. What You say is always a truth. What You say is always good. But some people think You did not rise from the dead. That is a big, big false. They also think if they trust in You then they have to give up good things. That is a false too. You only give good things. But Doctor Hemming does not think this way. He has no hope.

Doctor Hemming is sad.

That is because his family is dead.

That is why he does not believe in You.

Doctor Hemming does not know how much You love him. God, I think he thinks You hate him. Lots of people think this way, but they are wrong. It is sad. People want to believe they are right. They are stubborn. Stubborn is when a person will not think differently no matter what you say. These people are sometimes dumb, and sometimes sad. Doctor Hemming is sad. He thinks You hate him because his family died, because he is alive and he was the only one who lived. He would not be sad if he just stopped being stubborn. Then he would know You love him, God. If he knew, he would love You back. I think maybe he just needs to know that he is loved.

Emily loves him.

He loves Emily.

But they are not together.

I do not know why. When a person loves another person, they should be together for always. That is a truth. One time I asked Emily why Doctor Hemming is not her boyfriend. She laughed. She told me I was making things up. I said I was not because I saw them both kissing at his office. That was when I was Body Twenty. I know this because I wrote it down in the Calendar of Todd. That is when I saw them kissing. It is when I asked Emily why Doctor Hemming is not her boyfriend. When I told Emily this, her face got red and she laughed again but it was a different kind of laugh. Emily laughs this way when she burps on accident. It is quick and her face gets red and she sweats. She told me that was a private moment between her and Charlie. Then I asked who Charlie was. Emily said that

Charlie is Doctor Hemming and it was a private moment and not for me. So then I asked her again why Charlie is not her boyfriend. Emily said it is because Charlie is very sad. I told Emily I did not understand this. Then Emily said it is because Charlie loved his family so much. She said Charlie is still sad. I said to her that they should get married and we could be family. Emily cried and left the room when I said that, so now I do not ask things like this anymore. But I have seen them kiss a lot. And I have also heard them on the phone talking many times. But sometimes Emily does not want to see him. Then sometimes they do not talk for many months. But then they do. It is because they love each other.

I love Doctor Hemming too, but not like that.

I love him like he is my dad.

But he is not my dad.

Doctor Hemming calls me son. But I am not his son. Most of the time he calls me Todd. But sometimes he still calls me son. It would be cool and nice if Doctor Hemming were my dad. I would be his son. He would teach me to do cool things and then we could also go to the movies. But I am not his son because he had a son. His son died. And so did his wife. So did his daughter. They were shot by a bad person with a gun who was crazy. This was when I was Body Seven. I know this because I just do. Emily says he is always sad about it. If I were his son I would give him a hug. But I am not his son.

But I did give him a gift.

That is because today is his birthday.

Sons get their fathers gifts for their birthdays.

My gift to Doctor Hemming is a drawing. It is not a good drawing, but I did my best. It is a drawing of Doctor Hemming being smart. I drew him holding tubes around machines, but also with claws like Wolverine from X-Men because Doctor Hemming looks a lot like Wolverine except for the mustache because Wolverine does not have a mustache, but he does have claws and is angry like Doctor Hemming. Doctor Hemming is smart. He helped me make The Calendar of Todd. This is my calendar, God. I made it after the accident that made me not smart. It is my calendar of every day. When something happens, then I write it down in the Calendar of Todd. And that is because I forget things. But when I write it down in the Calendar of Todd, I know that the thing happened, and then I remember. I always make sure to write down the important things in The Calendar of Todd. Doctor Hemming told me to do this. My calendar is many pages long but I do not know how many pages because I did not count it. I always keep my calendar with me so I can look up things I forgot. It has Blue Days and Red Days and Gold Days and White Days and is called The Calendar of Todd. I am glad Doctor Hemming helped me make it. I put his birthday into my calendar. His birthday is on May First, Nineteen Sixty-Nine. He is fifty-five. I know Doctor Hemming is this old because Emily told me. That is why I drew him this drawing. I have never given Doctor Hemming anything before for his birthday, but I want to do this because I just do. I do not know why, but I am supposed to give Doctor Hemming this picture for his birthday. Sometimes people just need to know someone cares about them. Then they stop being sad all the time. I will give it to him the next time I see him. But I drew it for You too, God.

That is so You could see.

I wanted You to see Doctor Hemming.

I know You see everything.

But I want You to see him good. I think if we pray for people, You might see them better. That is because sometimes people do not pray for themselves, so it is my job to pray for them too. That is why I drew the picture, God, so You could see Doctor Hemming good. It is like a prayer. It is not words, but it is still a prayer. I do not know what I want to say, but I know You know. I want to pray something for Doctor Hemming. I pray he and Emily get married and are happy. God, this is important so I am going to write this one down in the Calendar of Todd and mark it. I am marking it blue because it is a Blue Day today which is Thursday, May Twenty-Third, Two Thousand and Twenty Four. It is important so I am writing it in big blue marker in a big blue circle so I know where to find it. This is the right prayer. Maybe it is not. I do not know. But it is okay, because You know. I know this because You are God who made all people. You see all people and their hearts. That is why I pray for Doctor Hemming. I pray You see him because he is in a big hurt. You see people who are in a big hurt.

And I pray You see me too.

Seven

PASTOR NATE'S CRUSADE

God, my pastor is Pastor Nate.

He is a good pastor.

He is not like others.

Pastor Nate is cool. He is forty-seven. I know this because he told me. He also likes sneakers. I know this because he told me and also I have seen him wear them. He is a cool dresser. He does not dress like other pastors. He wears jeans and t-shirts and sneakers. Sometimes we talk about sneakers. Pastor Nate teaches me things because he is my teacher. He teaches me stuff at church and the name of our church is called Morning Church. He has always been my teacher since after I said Jesus Christ is my Lord and Savior the day I died. When I came back to life, he said he would be my teacher. He helps me read the Bible and always tells me what things really mean if I do not understand. One time I did not understand You were God and Jesus Christ and the Holy Spirit. But he helped me understand. He said we cannot see You because You are the Ultimate Supreme Being. He said You became Jesus Christ who we could see who is also a human and God. He said the Holy Spirit is Your Spirit and the Third Person of the Holy Trinity. He said Jesus Christ saved me and loves me. It is a truth. Pastor Nate also teaches Ernie and Ira. He teaches many people. Once every month he takes me and Ernie and Ira to the movies. We get pizza after. Sometimes, we get burgers, but mostly we get pizza. Pastor Nate does this because he is our friend. Also, he likes Captain America, and looks like him too.

Pastor Nate is happy.

His family is in Heaven with You.

This is why he loves You.

Pastor Nate says he knows how much You love him. But he says we never really know. That is because You are too big for us to understand. But he knows You love him and I know too. He knows You love him even though his family is in Heaven. His whole family got shot. It was bad. They were shot by a bad person with a gun who was crazy. This happened when I was Body Seven. Pastor Nate talks about it sometimes. He is still sad. But he is not mad anymore. He said to me and other people that he tried to kill himself after his family died, but then he did not. He said he was about to and God stopped him by making him trip in his room into his bookshelf, and that is when the Bible fell on his head and opened up to one page and Pastor Nate saw one verse and it was this verse. Here is the verse. Yet the Lord longs to be gracious to you; therefore He will rise up to show you compassion, for the Lord is a God of justice, blessed are all who wait for him! This is from Isaiah 30:18. Pastor Nate read this verse and says that is how God spoke to him. Pastor Nate says that God speaks in many ways but you can always trust when God speaks to you from the Bible because the Bible is a truth. Pastor Nate said that after he read that verse his doorbell rang and someone left him a meatloaf. Pastor Nate told me that he hates meatloaf. But he ate it because he had not eaten much for a month. Pastor Nate said that is when he decided not to kill himself, because God had compassion on him. He said later he found out the person who left the meatloaf was Nora. Nora is his wife now. Pastor Nate said this is how he knows Jesus Christ loves him.

Nora is pretty.

She is Korean.

Pastor Nate is white.

Some people do not like that Nora is Korean. Emily says this is why some people do not go to Morning Church, but this has never made any truth to me because Nora has love in her heart. Emily says some people do not like Nora because of this. This makes me mad because it makes no truth. Do people not understand that God has made all people everywhere? It is sad when Christian people do that because it means they are not doing what God told them to do. What God says is to love all people always. They are hating. The only thing to hate is evil. Evil is a big lie. But love is a bigger truth. And love is not weak. Love means sometimes you have to fight. One time when I was Body Nine I yelled at a person holding a mean sign outside of our church. He was screaming bad things because Nora is Korean and there are not many Korean people here. I yelled back at him and did not like him. He did this on a Blue Day Tuesday. I know this because I wrote it down in The Calendar of Todd. Nora told me she forgave the person and I had to also forgive. Nora said that we must forgive. She said love does not mean you will not get angry and it does not mean you should not defend yourself and it does not mean you should not fight to do what God says. She said God gets angry too, and God will judge. But she said love means we must forgive. She forgives those kinds of people because they have a hurt. That is love.

Love is a good thing.

Love is the best thing.

I am commanded to love all people.

Sometimes I do not love me. Because I do not forgive myself. I cannot forgive me. I asked Nora about the crazy man with a gun a long time ago who shot and killed all those people. She said she forgives him too. But she said that lots of other people will never forgive that man. I forgave that crazy person because I did even though he did a bad thing and hurt many people. But I do not forgive myself, and I wish I could, but I am very mad at myself.

Pastor Nate is not mad.

Pastor Nate forgives the crazy man.

That is how Pastor Nate got his mission.

Pastor Nate calls it a crusade. Pastor Nate wants to change gun laws in America. Many people hate him because of this. One time he was talking about it and someone got mad. It was after church and this person yelled at Pastor Nate. His name was Shane. This was when I was Body Ten. I know it because I wrote it down in the Calendar of Todd. Shane said he had a good right to kill someone if someone broke into his house. So I raised my hand when Shane said this because I had a question. Then Shane and Pastor Nate and everybody else laughed a lot. I do not know why. Then Shane asked me what my question was. I asked Shane who broke into his house. He said nobody did, it was just in case. So I asked him why he would want to kill someone. Shane said he did not want to kill anyone. Then I said if nobody broke into his house and he did not want to kill anyone, I asked why he needed a gun. Shane told me that it was just in case. Then I asked, in case of what. He said in case someone broke into his house. This makes no truth. Shane said I would not get it because I could not understand because the world is complicated. But I understood. I even said that I understood. And I said that it is okay to defend yourself but it is not okay to kill because only God is allowed to do that. Shane said but what if someone breaks into his house. I asked why he could not shoot that person in the foot and not kill them. Shane laughed. It was not funny. He is not a policeman. He is Shane who lives way up on the hill with his dog. I said this to him. He laughed. Then everyone laughed. But I did not. I thought it was serious. Pastor Nate says it is serious. And it is. But then Shane asked me what I would do if someone came after me or Emily with a gun, and I said if someone did that I would hurt them bad and maybe kill them, but then my eyes hurt and got wet and I cried but I did not know why and Emily swore at Shane and Shane said he was sorry many times and then I said, okay I do not know why I am crying.

    Shane is both right and wrong.

    Pastor Nate is both right and wrong.

    The truth is that evil is in the world.

    Life is a complicated and serious thing, but I understand. Pastor Nate made a complicated and serious choice to do a crusade. It is so complicated and serious that Pastor Nate says people send him mail to say they want him to die. But he will not die. God, I just remembered a verse. It is a good verse. Here is the verse. I will not die, but live, and will proclaim what the Lord has done. It is from Psalm 118:17. I was supposed to die long ago, but I did not. Because I will live and not die. Pastor Nate says when I speak Your Promises is when big time miracles happen. So I will speak Your Promises. I will never give up. Pastor Nate says he will never give up either. He says life is a complicated and serious thing.

    I think so too.

Eight

ERNIE & IRA

God, I have two friends.

Their names are Ernie and Ira.

Ernie is like me, Ira is not.

They are my good friends. Ernie is slow like me, but not dumb like me. Ernie is actually smart. I am dumb and slow. But Ernie is smart and slow. Ernie is mentally retarded, but Ernie is not dumb. If someone is mentally retarded, then they are not dumb at all. That is how some people are made. I was not made that way. I was made smart, but I got dumb. It is my fault. But Ernie has no fault. He is smart. Ernie can read and he likes books, but it takes him a long time to do this. It does not take Ira much time to to read books because Ira is a smart person. Ira is not like me, and he is not like Ernie. Ira is normal. But Ira has issues and does not like people. I know this because Ira said he has issues and he said that he does not like people. Ira says people are evil swear word mongers. I do not know what an evil swear word monger is, but it sounds bad, so I do not want to know. Ira also says me and Ernie are not evil swear word mongers. That is why Ira decided to be our friend, because he says other people are evil, and the world is evil and full of evil, but we are pure. We are all friends and we are all the same body age and we do things together sometimes.

One thing we do is meet.

We always meet on Red Day Wednesdays.

God, I will tell you how I met Ernie and Ira.

This is what happened. We met when I was Body Twenty. I wrote down the day. It was on Red Day Wednesday, May Twenty-Fifth, Two Thousand and Eleven. We have been friends for thirteen entire whole years since then. We met because Pastor Nate asked us to. Pastor Nate said I needed to have friends because I did not have any. My only friend was Izzy. Izzy and me talked every day, but then we did not because she had to go away to Morning Home. Me and Izzy talk twice a week. But me and Ernie and Ira talk three entire times a week. It is because Pastor Nate brings them to church on Red Day Wednesdays. I also see them on Blue Day Tuesdays and Blue Day Thursdays when I see Izzy at Morning Home. That is because Ernie and Ira live at Morning Home too. Pastor Nate met them a long time ago. Pastor Nate goes to Morning Home every Red Day Monday and he talks to the people there. He tells them about Jesus Christ and the Promises of God and it is good because people listen, like Ernie and Ira and Izzy. They all trust in You. And one day after Pastor Nate talked about You he asked Ernie and Ira if they wanted to make a new friend, and they said yes. Pastor Nate asked Izzy too, but Izzy knew me and also Izzy could not leave because they never let Izzy leave unless it is with the Morning Home guards. They always watch her and it is weird. But what happened is Pastor Nate brought Ernie and Ira to the church and it is where we became good friends.

 I know many things about Ernie and Ira.

 Because we became friends.

 But they are more than friends.

 They are like my brothers. I do not have brothers, but if I did, it would be Ernie and Ira. And this is how I know many things about Ernie and Ira because if you have brothers, you know many things about them.

 Here are some things I know.

 Ernie and Ira live at Morning Home because Ernie cannot take care of himself and Ira is crazy. Ira says he is not a crazy person, but people think he is and it is why he lives at Morning Home. Ira is not mean. He is good. Ira says his parents sent him there and he is not allowed to leave. That is because when Ira was seventeen, he almost killed a policeman because Ira was on drugs. Ira said the policeman was mean and he got mad and they got in a fight and Ira hurt him bad and then Ira had to go to jail, but they said he did not have to go to jail if Ira promised to live at Morning Home forever. Ira wishes he never did it. Now Ira will have to live at Morning Home for the rest of his life. Ernie also has to live at Morning Home. Ernie says his parents sent him to Morning Home because they could not take care of him good. They are dead now. Ernie said his parents paid for him to be at Morning Home for his whole life. Ernie says his mom loved him very much. He loved his mom too. He wishes his mom were here. Ira also loves his mom, but he is mad because he has to live here.

I know other things about Ernie and Ira too.

I know Ira is black and Korean and Jewish. Ira says he is the biggest minority in the world. He says it means he is a small person, but that is not a truth because Ira is a large person. Ira has a muscle on his arm that is bigger than my head. That is just one muscle. He has many muscles and is tall and says it is one reason why people do not like him. He says he is a scary man. But when he said that, I told him he is not a scary man at all. He asked me why. I said that he is a like a nice, big brother. Big brothers are not scary. They are nice. Ira rubbed my hair when I said that and gave me a hug with one arm. Ernie saw Ira give me a hug with one arm so then Ernie laughed and he came over and hugged us both and then Ira said, Okay buddy I get it.

I think we are like brothers.

Brothers know many things about each other. They know many things about me and I know many things about them. I said we are like Spider-Man and Ben Reilly and Kaine in the Spider-Man Clone Saga. They did not get it. So I told them that in the Spider-Man Clone Saga, Peter Parker is cloned and one clone is called Ben Reilly and the other clone is called Kaine, and at first they are enemies but then they are like brothers, sort of. They sort of fight too. But it does not matter because they are the same but not and are brothers and friends. And I said that is like us. They still did not understand so I said we are like knights for King Arthur. They understood this. We are all friends and take care of each other and are happy with each other. We all know things about each other and also we know each other real good.

We are like brothers.

Nine
BLUE DAYS WITH IZZY

God, I have another friend too.

Her name is Izzy.

I love her.

Izzy has been my friend my entire whole life. She was my friend when I was smart and she was my friend when I became dumb. She has been my friend ever since I can remember. When I was Body Six, Emily took a photo of Izzy and me and then Izzy wrote on on the photo. It said Izzy and Todd for always. She drew a heart on it. She said we were going to get married. We will not get married anymore. That is because I am dumb now. But I saved the photo of us. Emily said me and Izzy were born at the same time at the same hospital. I did not believe this. I told Emily I did not believe this. Emily said she could prove it and then she proved it with papers. It is a truth. It said me and Izzy were born Saturday, July Twenty-Seventh, Nineteen Ninety-One. We were born at exactly the same time which is Three Thirty-Three in the afternoon. Emily told me that me and Izzy have known each other for always. I am like Peter Pan and Izzy is like Wendy. Izzy is not my *best* friend, she is my *always* friend.

Izzy is pretty.

She has always been pretty.

Izzy will always be pretty.

Izzy is pretty in her face and in her heart. Some people are only pretty in their face. She is pretty in her heart too. I know because of many things that

Izzy has told me that I wrote down in The Calendar of Todd. Some of these things she told me when I was smart and I remember. But some of these things she told me when I was dumb. One thing she said is she wanted to be President of the United States to stop wars. She said this after her brother died, because he was a soldier who went to war and he died. She said this when I was smart so I remember. That is one reason she is pretty in her heart. Another thing she said once is that she wanted to be a teacher for her whole life and be a writer. She said she wanted to teach little children because children are precious and need to be cared for. Izzy said she wanted to read them stories and love them and do that for always. This was after I became dumb so I wrote it down. Izzy said this on Thursday, May Thirteenth, Two Thousand and Four at Two in the afternoon. She has said many nice things like this. Also, she kept being my friend even after I became dumb. When I became dumb, Izzy would come to my house to play every day after she was done with school. We played many games. We played games I do not remember because I could not understand. But Izzy helped. We also played with my Star Wars toys and He-Man toys and G.I. Joe toys. Izzy liked to be Luke Skywalker the most and I liked to be He-Man. We played and read. But I could not read good, so Izzy read to me. She liked to read me lots and lots of books. She liked reading me King Arthur stories and Peter Pan stories from many of the books she had. Izzy took books from the library and had many King Arthur books and she read them all to me. I do not remember them, but I remember Izzy reading. She also took me to the movies. After I became dumb, we saw lots of movies together. We liked to go to the old movie theater because nobody went there. It was just us together and they showed us old movies. We liked all of them. And I wrote down all of the movies we liked. We liked The Shawshank Redemption and Forrest Gump and the Star Wars movies and Back to the Future Part I and Part II and Part III and Field of Dreams. There are more. Izzy held my hand when we watched movies. She was always nice to the people there. These are the reasons she is pretty in her heart.

When I see Izzy, it is a good day.

We have always seen each other.

Me and Izzy do not like not seeing each other.

Izzy always came to see me each day at three in the afternoon until she did not. It was Thursday, September Ninth, Two Thousand and Ten. I did not write this in the Calendar of Todd. That is because I remember. I remember because I just do. Izzy did not come to my house that day. I waited for a while, but Izzy did not come to my house. I asked Emily where Izzy was but Emily did not know. I waited in my room, but Izzy did not come. And I waited until dinner time and Emily came into my room. Emily was crying and I asked her why she was crying. Emily said that Izzy tried to hurt herself, and that she was real sick. That did not make any truth to me. Izzy was not sick. When you are sick you make yourself better. If a person is sick and they hurt themselves that will just make it worse. It made no truth. If Izzy was sick she would make herself better, she would not hurt herself. Izzy would not do that. Also, if a person is sick they should talk to You, God, and You would make them not sick. Izzy trusts in You, God. She would have asked You for help and You would have helped. It still does not make any truth to me and makes me mad because it is hard to see Izzy now. Because her parents sent Izzy to live at Morning Home to be alone. We can no longer go to the movies together. She does not visit me anymore. I visit her. I go see Izzy on Blue Days. I go to Morning Home, but I do not like it. Emily does not like me going to Morning Home either and Emily told me I am not allowed to go. The first time I said I was going to Morning Home, Emily cried a lot.

I said, Emily, Why are you sad and crying?

She said, Because life is just like always so unfair.

I said, Emily, I do not understand.

She said, You can't go see Izzy.

I said, No.

Emily said, No.

Then I said, Yes.

Emily said, Stop and just listen, you cannot go see Izzy.

So I asked Emily why.

She said, Because the place is for the psycho deranged nutcase losers.

Then Emily said, You're not going.

I said, I have to go because I have to see Izzy every single day.

Emily said, No, you're not going, not now, not ever.

I said, Yes now yes always.

But then Emily said, No and that's final.

So I said I was going to go anyway.

Then Emily said I could not.

So I said I would only go on Blue Days.

She said, No, no, no, no, no, no and no.

Then I cried because I was sad.

Emily felt bad because she always feels bad when I cry. Then she said I could only go one Blue Day a week. I did not like that. But I said okay. Then I said we have to shake. Emily and me shook hands and I said I promised.

But I lied.

I go every Blue Day and sometimes even more. I did not tell Emily and she does not know. I will never tell her because she would be mad. She would be mad I hurt her and I love Emily. It is why I do not tell Emily. But I love Izzy too. Sometimes two things are a truth at the same time. That is a hard thing. Also I get to see Ernie and Ira when I go to Morning Home and they are happy when I see them. But I wish I did not ever have to go to Morning Home. When I go there it is always sad. Sometimes when I go see Izzy, it is the same as when I walk into a room after Emily was crying. When I walk into a room after Emily has been crying, I do not see Emily crying, but I know she was. Morning Home is like that. Every time I go see Izzy at Morning Home it is dark in the sky and I just know people have been crying.

I will see Izzy tomorrow.

I will bring her my Luke Skywalker toy.

I love her.

PRESENTING A MINI MOVIE EPISODE OF
THE ADVENTURES OF TODD

IN

TODD
and
THE
TIME
LOOP

A Time Travel EPIC
Part I
A Mini Movie by Todd

written for the screen by Todd Carpenter on Friday July 4th, 1997

OVER BLACK.

The sound of film rolling in a projector while a flicker of red and white and black along with a split-second image of perforated celluloid over the screen and --

A WATCH FACE.

Tick, tick, tick -- stop on **three o'clock exactly**.
A child's small finger taps it. That finger belongs to --

TODD.

Seven-years-old, tapping his watch. He ignores and continues on his way, walking a small town bridge in Morning, New York. He ambles along the pedestrian walkway. Sunlight shines in the waning afternoon daylight. He hikes up his backpack on his back and tightens his baseball cap.

And in a deep voice --

                    NARRATOR (V.O.)
               Todd was a normal, happy, child
               prodigy with dreams of becoming an
               astronaut. He was neat and cool
               and also really popular.

Some guy in a car drives past Todd and beeps the horn --

                    SOME GUY IN A CAR
               Yo, Todd, you're really popular!

Todd waves as the guy in the car drives onward.
A lone newspaper page flies by Todd's face, caught in the wind's gust. **A WHITE HORSE** gallops over to Todd and waits for a moment -- Todd stares at the animal in confusion -- the horse moves on and races away.

Todd shrugs it off.

                    NARRATOR (V.O.)
               All was well in Todd's world.

FLASH --

                    NARRATOR (V.O.)
               Until World War Three.

A SUPERNOVA BRIGHT FLARE IN THE DISTANCE. Todd stops and covers his eyes. He looks far off toward the mountains where **a mushroom cloud** rises high into the sky --

FLASH-FLASH-FLASH --

More atomic blasts, two flares far away, one blast nearby --
a blast wave comes closer, closer, closer --
Todd grips the bridge railing as --

TODD.

Opening his eyes, still gripping the railing. Sounds of cars driving by, the wind blows, everything seems totally normal. He looks at his watch -- tick, tick, tick -- **stop on three o'clock exactly**.

Some guy in a car drives past Todd and beeps the horn --

>   SOME GUY IN A CAR
>   Yo, Todd, you're really popular!

Todd gives a half-hearted wave as the guy in the car passes. A lone newspaper page flies by Todd's face, caught in the wind. **THE WHITE HORSE** returns, galloping the walkway over to Todd and waits for another moment -- Todd stares at the animal in confusion again -- the horse races away once more. Todd watches the horse leave with a skeptic glance.

The boy's expression turns grim --

>   TODD
>   Oh no, I'm caught in a time loop.

FLASH -- A NUCLEAR EXPLOSION IN THE DISTANCE --
Todd grips the bridge railing once more --

>   NARRATOR (V.O.)
>   Now caught in a time loop, he must
>   figure out how to stop the end of
>   the world --

TODD.

Opening his eyes again. Everything seems back to normal. He looks at his watch, which reads **two fifty-nine**.

>   TODD
>   I've only got one minute.

>   NARRATOR (V.O.)
>   In only one minute.

Todd RUNS, fast, fast, fast, but not fast enough as --
some guy in a car drives past Todd and beeps the horn --

                    SOME GUY IN A CAR
          Yo, Todd, you're really popular!

                    TODD
          Thanks, man!

The lone newspaper page flies by Todd's face and --
THE WHITE HORSE gallops past him going far faster --

                    TODD
          I'm too late!

FLASH -- A NUCLEAR EXPLOSION IN THE DISTANCE --
Todd ducks and covers as the blast wave comes closer and --

TODD.

Opening his eyes once more. The world looks tranquil.
He looks at his watch, which reads **two fifty-nine**.

He sighs.

                    TODD
          Great.

THE WHITE HORSE RETURNS. It stops in front of Todd --
this time Todd hops on the horse and rides away **FAST** --

                    NARRATOR (V.O.)
          For any normal human, this would be
          impossible, but now Todd can go
          really, really fast.

                    TODD
          I'm riding really, really fast.

                    NARRATOR (V.O.)
          Due to special powers from the
          previous nuclear explosions, his
          new horse can gallop at super
          speeds --

                    TODD
          It must be due to special powers
          from the previous nuclear
          explosions that can make my horse
          run at super speeds --

The horse neighs, loud, as if in agreement with Todd's
assessment of these newfound powers --

                    TODD
          You'll need a name, horse.
          So I will call you --

A crack of thunder in the sky -- it catches Todd's attention.

                    NARRATOR (V.O.)
          Thunder Son.

                    TODD
          Thunder Son.

Some guy in a car drives past Todd and beeps the horn --

                    SOME GUY IN A CAR
          Yo, Todd, you're really popular!

                    TODD
          No!

                    SOME GUY IN A CAR
          Yeah you totally are!

The lone newspaper page flies by Todd's face --

FLASH --

ANOTHER ATOMIC BOMB --

TODD.

Opening his eyes to an ordinary world. His watch reads two fifty-nine -- here comes **THUNDER SON** the white horse. Todd jumps on and they ride away, faster than ever before --

FAST --

FAST --

FAST --

The world becomes streaks around Todd and Thunder Son --

                    NARRATOR (V.O.)
          Now with his superior horse,
          Thunder Son, Todd must ride so fast
          that he will go back in time to
          warn the President of the United
          States of the impending
          thermonuclear war.

                    TODD
          Thunder Son, with your special
          speed powers we'll have to ride
          back in time to warn the President
          of the United States of the
          impending thermonuclear war.

A HIGHWAY.

Todd rides faster than all the cars on the road weaving in
and out, traveling to --

PENNSYLVANIA AVENUE.

Todd and Thunder Son stop before the gates of the WHITE HOUSE.
Some new guy in a car drives past Todd and beeps the horn --

                    SOME NEW GUY IN A CAR
          Yo, man, you seem really popular!

                    TODD
          Oh come on!

FLASH -- another nuclear bomb blows not far away,
the ensuing mushroom cloud towers over Todd and the blast
wave heads directly for him --

TODD.

Opening his eyes once more to a normal world. His watch reads
two fifty-nine -- on cue, **THUNDER SON** arrives. Todd leaps on
the horse and off they go, riding faster than before --
so fast that the background becomes all white while Todd
rides with a strenuous grin on his face --

                    NARRATOR (V.O.)
          Can he ever make it in time?

                    TODD
          I have to make it in time!

FLASH -- a thermonuclear explosions turns the screen dark as --

                                        CUT TO BLACK.

                    NARRATOR (V.O.)
          Find out this summer, time
          traveling to a theater near you.
          Rated PG thirteen.

                                        BACK TO:

TODD.

Opening his eyes a final time. He looks at his watch, which again reads **two fifty-nine**.

He sighs.

A car speeds toward him, same as always.

                    TODD
          Here we go again.
          Some guy in a car.

Except it's a sleek, shining black car with black wheels driving at about one-hundred miles per hour -- SCREECHING TO A HALT RIGHT IN FRONT OF TODD.

The window rolls down --

An empty driver's seat.

                    TODD
          What is this? What are you?

                  THE BLACK CAR
              (in a robotic voice)
          Hello, Todd. I am Thunder Son.
          We have to go back in time.
          Again.

Todd's eyes go wide and he smiles as --

                                      CUT TO BLACK.
                                          AGAIN.

TODD and THE TIME LOOP

FOREVERLAND ENTERTAINMENT PRESENTS
A FOREVERLAND ENTERTAINMENT PRODUCTION "TODD AND THE TIME LOOP" A TODD CARPENTER MINI MOVIE
STARRING TODD CARPENTER THUNDER SON SOME GUY IN A CAR NUCLEAR BOMBS ANOTHER GUY IN A CAR THE WRISTWATCH
DESIGN BY TODD
DISTRIBUTED BY FOREVERLAND ENTERTAINMENT

Ten

A
NEW
HOPE

God, my town is called Morning, New York.

Morning is where I live.

Morning is where I will die.

I have lived in Morning my entire whole life since Saturday, July Twenty-Seventh, Nineteen Ninety-One at Three Thirty-Three in the afternoon, and I will live here the rest of my entire whole life until I die. That is life. Emily said this once a long time ago. She said I will live the rest of my entire whole life in Morning, New York. When I asked her why, she said, That's life. Then she said, Look, that's just where you live, Todd, and it's where you're gonna die, and it's where I'm gonna die too and that's just life, so I suggest you get used to it and just move on. I did not understand. I like Morning. I like where I live. And then my head hurt bad and then I cried. Emily asked why I was crying, but I could not answer because this happened when I was Body Seven, but after I was no longer smart and when I became dumb. I wanted to say things but I did not know how. I still do not know how to say these things, but I remember I did not like what she said, and I did not like the way she said it, and I did not like how she looked when she said it and I also did not like the way she was putting groceries into the refrigerator either when she said this. She looked angry and had no hope. God, I just had a thought and now I understand. Emily did not have hope then. I did not like this. To have no hope is a bad thing. No hope makes good people sad and bad people worse. Some people have hope, but many do not. That is life.

Some days I have not much hope.

But I still have more than no hope.

And today I had hope and happiness.

Today was a Blue Day. Blue Days are on Tuesdays. Tuesdays are always Blue Days. In The Calendar of Todd there are Blue Days and Red Days and White Days and Gold Days. There are no other days, so there are no other colors and these are the best colors I have picked. Blue Days are on Tuesday and Thursday. Red Days are on Monday and Wednesday and Friday. White Days are on Saturday. And Gold Days are on Sunday. This is the way my calendar looks. Some things I do on Blue Days, and some things I do on Red Days. Some things I do on White Days, and some things I do on Gold Days. But there are some things I do on All Days, like watching movies, because it is fun. On All Days I also pray to You, God, but this is sometimes hard and that is why I write to You too. I cannot remember all the things on All Days and that is why I use The Calendar of Todd. Today was a Blue Day, so today I went to see Doctor Hemming, Pastor Nate, and Izzy. Blue Days are my favorite. So are Red Days and White Days and Gold Days. All Days are my favorite. But Blue Days are my most favorite.

God, this is how my day began.

This is also how All Days begin.

Some days it is easy, some days it is hard.

God, I woke up today, but it was hard. Waking up is not hard, but the part after waking up is hard. Because as soon as I wake up I have thoughts and they are not always good thoughts. They are the voices I do not want. That is what happened when I woke up. I woke up at Five Fifteen this morning. This is the time I wake up on All Days. I opened my eyes and the voices came. They said bad things. I did not like what they said, and I will not write it because it is bad. So I got out of bed and got on my knees and I prayed. It did not go good. God, You know this. The voices spoke when I prayed. I could not think, so I could not pray so I stopped. I did not want You to hear and get mad at me. I did not know what to think. I could not know if the voices were mine. I do not think they were, but I do not know how I would know, so I hope they were not. This made me cry. I cried because if I cannot talk right to You then I do not want to live. I also cried because I knew You heard the voices too. If they are mine, then I am in trouble. So I prayed that I was sorry and I asked for forgiveness for my bad thoughts. This is when I remembered in the Bible it says, The Spirit himself intercedes for us through wordless groans. This is from Romans 8:26. I never knew what this meant. So one time a long time ago I asked Pastor Nate what it meant and he said it means The Spirit of God prays for us, because we do not know what or how to pray, so The Spirit helps us. So I remembered this and I had more hope. I do not have hope in me sometimes. But I know You look at me and have hope.

You see me as the me I am supposed to be.

That is when I looked in the mirror and saw me. God, I am still a boy and I am small. I have not grown older. This is what I see because it is a truth. But I had a thought. My thought was I do not know why people do not see what I see. I see me who is seven and it is a truth. But I am also thirty-three and that is a truth too. I do not see this. But that is how people see me. They do not see me as a seven-year-old. I had another thought after this. My new thought was, I wonder what I would look like as a person who is Body Thirty-Three. I do not know because it is not what I see. I just see me, and I like me.

Sometimes I do not like me.

But I know You like me always.

This is a good feeling.

And it gave me more hope. So I did more things that give me hope when I woke up. God, when I do something and do it good, it gives me hope. So I made my bed since I can do this good. I make my bed on All Days. Then I went to my closet and got my clothes. I do this on All Days too. I put out my Rocky Clothes and my Blue Day Clothes. My Rocky Clothes are the same on All Days. My Rocky clothes are gray sweatpants and a gray sweatshirt like in the cool movie Rocky. My Blue Day clothes are jeans, a blue T-shirt, a blue button shirt, and a blue hat. My Blue Day hat is a Los Angeles Dodgers hat, because it is blue, and because I like baseball, and also I think it is a cool hat. But my favorite team is the Boston Red Sox. I only wear my Red Sox hat on Red Days because it is has red on it. On White Days I wear my Blue Day hat and on Gold Days I wear my Red Day hat because I do not own any white hats or any gold hats and also gold hats suck.

So I set my Blue Day hat on my backpack and I packed my backpack with the things I will need for my Blue Day. God, these are all the same things I pack in my backpack on All Days. I pack my Bible, The Calendar of Todd, my allowance, my watch, my Polaroid camera and my Polaroid photos, my mixtapes, my comic books, The Once and Future King by a person named T.H. White, Peter Pan by a person named J.M. Barrie and my pen, and my pencil and my notebooks, so I can write to You. I also packed my Luke Skywalker toy for Izzy because I said I would. I did this and got on my knees and prayed again by my bed. I said thank You, God, because You woke me up and give me life. I said, Please keep me safe and please keep me from getting lost, and please let me have a good day and not a bad day. Once I did all these things I had more hope.

I need lots of hope before I do anything.

This is why I talk to You. You give me hope. When I have hope, I can do my moves. So I went into the backyard with my Rocky clothes on. I also do this on All Days. I do jumping jacks and sit-ups and pushups and I run in circles, and I do this for ten songs, which is one side of one mixtape on my Rocky mixtape and that is how I know when to stop. Sometimes I have to stop because I am out of breath, sometimes I do not. Today I did not have to stop. Today I did all the moves that Rocky does when he does his moves in Rocky, except the hard ones because I am not allowed to do those. I just do my moves that Emily says I am allowed to do. This makes me hungry so I always eat lots of eggs and a bunch of toast after I do my moves. Then I shower because I am gross.

I shower every single day.

Sometimes I shower twice.

God, I am a clean person.

I am ready to leave home at Seven Forty on All Days, but I am afraid first. This happens every day when I get to the door. I get afraid. I do not know why. But I am afraid of lots of things. I am afraid of being lost. I am afraid I will do something wrong and You will get mad at me, but I do not know why. I am afraid of things I do not know and there are many things I do not know. I do not want to be afraid, but it happens, and I cannot be afraid so I just have to fix it. So then I go to my room and set my alarm for Eight Thirty because I have to leave then and I am always not scared by that time. So I sit at my desk and read my Bible with highlighters. I have blue and yellow highlighters. Sometimes I highlight verses and sometimes I do not. Sometimes I am scared about things, and then I read a verse and You fix it. Sometimes I read a verse and I am afraid I did something wrong, but I do not know what I did. That makes me cry because then sometimes I think I am in trouble and if You are mad, it is bad. Sometimes this happens and I get so afraid I do not move and do not think and then I do nothing. This is the worst kind of afraid. It makes me want to throw up. But I always hold it in and I have not thrown up in a long time because of afraidness. When this happens I remember in the Bible it says, The Lord himself goes before you and will be with you; he will never leave you nor forsake you. Do not be afraid; do not be discouraged. God, this one is from Deuteronomy 31:8. I always remember that. This happened today because I thought about hell. I got afraid. I did not move and did not think. I was shaking because hell is scary. But I remembered when I am afraid I should not be. So I was not afraid. And also I remembered I am not going to hell. And my alarm went off so it was time to go. Then I was not afraid and I left my room. Because I was trusting You will never leave me. That is what happens when I go places. This is how I go out of my room.

If I trust in You, I can go anywhere.

The place I went this morning was the car. That is because every Blue Day at Nine in the morning, Emily brings me to Doctor Hemming. On Red Days I do not have to be anywhere and I walk places and I sometimes get lost. On Blue Days I have to get in the car and Emily takes me to Doctor Hemming. This is one reason why I like Blue Days but it is not the only reason I like Blue Days.

I like Blue Days for many reasons.

Mostly I like Blue Days because I get to listen to my Blue Day mixtape which has Journey and Bruce Springsteen on it. I like my Red Day mixtape too, and my White Day Mixtape and my Gold Day mixtape, but I really like my Blue Day mixtape. Sometimes I listen to all my mixtapes in one day and break the rules but it is okay because I am not sinning. Today Emily was mad and did not like my mixtape on the way to see Doctor Hemming. I put my mixtape in the tape player and she took it out. So I put the tape back in and she took it back out.

She said, I don't want to listen to eighties music right now.

I said, Why?

She said, Because I just don't.

I said, Why?

She said, Because I don't okay?

I said, But why?

She said, Just do what I say.

I said, Why?

She said, Todd, I don't want to listen to it.

I said, Why?

She said, Why do you keep asking why?

I said, Because I want to know why.

She said, Why what?

I said, Why do you not want to listen to it?

Emily got mad and made a scrunched face and her face got red and she yelled and said to me, Can you stop for like one second?

So I stopped for one second.

Then I said, Why?

Emily yelled again and said, Stop it now.

She turned on the radio loud and we did not talk because she was mad. I did not do anything wrong so I did not deserve her madness. But I was not mad at her. Also I did not get to listen to my Blue Day mixtape on the way to see Doctor Hemming. But there was a song on the radio that I liked and I asked Emily what it was, and she said the song was Van Morrison.

I asked, What is Van Morrison?

Emily told me that Van Morrison is a person. So I asked Emily if she could put Van Morrison the person on my mixtape and then she said, Whatever. This means she will, but she does not want to. It is okay, because it will get done and soon I will listen to a new song by Van Morrison on my Blue Day mixtape.

God, I like music.

I am glad You invented it.

I am always listening to music.

Sometimes I listen to the same song over and over because I forgot I just listened to it. Other times I listen to the same song over and over because I like it. But then also I listen to the same song over and over because I forget that I just listened to it. I think I just said that. I just read what I wrote and saw that I said that, but it is also a truth so I am going to leave it. I have been forgetting a lot. It makes me afraid. I do not want to remember that I forget. So I listen to music to forget. I listened to music when we got to Doctor Hemming, because we always have to wait before he tells us to go into the room. So that is when I listen to my mixtape. My mixtape has many songs. I heard these songs and I told Emily I liked them and she put them on my mixtapes. Some songs she puts on there without me telling her to do it and I like it. There is lots of Bruce Springsteen and Journey. I also listen to Prince and Don Henley. I listen to praise music too. Sometimes when the voices are loud I listen to praise music louder. Praise music is good. Lots of times I forget what I am listening to so when I listen I am surprised. I forget a lot lately. I think that is why I have to keep coming back to see Doctor Hemming. Emily and I were waiting in the outside part and I was listening to my mixtape and that is when Doctor Hemming came out.

He said, Hello, Todd, what are you listening to?

But I did not hear him because I had my headphones on and my tape was playing, so I took my headphones off. I said, I did not hear you.

He said, I asked what you were listening to.

But I forgot and told him I did not remember. I have been forgetting. Then he smiled and said it was okay and we walked into the other room. I played my song again because I forgot what it was, but I do not remember anymore.

I have been coming here for a long time.

I know this because I checked The Calendar of Todd.

The first time I came here I was Body Seven. Emily held my hand when we went inside. I was Body Seven, and Emily was Nineteen, and I told Emily I was afraid and she said she was afraid for me too. The first time I came here, Emily brought me into the white room with a desk and two chairs. It is the same white room they have always put me in since I became not smart. I did not always have to be here as much as I do now. I know because I looked in The Calendar of Todd.

When I first became not smart, I only had to be here once every three months. Then when I was Body Ten, I had to be here once every two months. Then when I was Body Fifteen, I had to be here once every month. When I was Body Twenty, I had to be here once every two weeks. When I was Body Twenty-Eight, I had to be here once every week. Then when I was Body Thirty, I had to be here twice a week. And I still have to be here twice a week. I know this because I looked in The Calendar of Todd. Every time I am here I have to play with blocks and make them fit. Sometimes Doctor Hemming tells me things and tells me to say them back to him and sometimes I remember and sometimes I do not. Last week they put me on my back and I had to be still for a long time and they put me in a machine and took pictures of my brain. Today, I played with the blocks. Doctor Hemming was not watching. Neither was Emily. They were talking. Emily told me to listen to my music so I did, but I had to flip my mixtape, and when I flipped my mixtape, I heard them. Doctor Hemming said things that made me afraid.

    He said, More tests.

    He said, Prepare yourself.

    He said, I know this will be hard.

    He said, Morning Institute.

    Emily said, He can't go there, not yet.

    Emily looked at me and saw me watching so she told me to listen to my music. So I flipped my mixtape. But I watched them. Emily looked at her feet. She shook her head a lot too. But I did not know why. We left the white room and Emily held my hand when we walked out and I knew something was wrong.

    Emily holds my hand sometimes.

    Like when we watch a movie and it is scary.

    When she does this I know she loves me.

    Emily let go of my hand when we got to her car, but she still loves me. She told me it was time for me to go see Pastor Nate and that she had to go to work and that she would be home late. I said okay, but it was not okay. I do not like this because when Emily is home late I have to eat peanut butter and jelly or eggs since that is all I know how to make. Emily kissed me on my cheek and said to have a good day. And some of her hair was on my shoulder because she has lots of brown hair and it is always falling out. I am always finding her hair. It is all over the place. I am always finding her hairs on the couch and in the bathroom and in the kitchen and on the floor and her hairs are also always on me and it has always been this way since I was smart. Emily says her hair falls out because she is skinny. I do not think this is a truth. I think Emily likes to talk about how she is skinny because it makes her feel good and that is okay because I want Emily to always feel good. She has felt sad for a while. She cries a lot too and does not think I know, but I know. So sometimes I tell her she looks pretty even on Saturday mornings when it is a false, but it is still a truth. Emily has a pretty face, and pretty teeth and she is skinny and has pretty hair which is always falling on me and everywhere else in our home, and one time in my food.

Emily took the hairs off my shoulder.

I said, Emily I love you.

She was sad. She looked down at her feet and wiped her eyes. Then she looked up and she was crying. And she hugged me tight and she cried some more.

I said, Why are you sad, Emily?

All she said was, I love you too.

Then Emily got in her car and drove to work.

God, Emily works at the hospital where she helps people. She is a nurse. I have no job. Emily says this is okay because I do not need one. Emily says my job is to be myself and trust Jesus Christ for everything else.

God, sometimes I call You by Jesus.

Sometimes I call You by God.

Sometimes I call You God Almighty.

God, it is a serious thing when people use Your Name and call You by Jesus Christ. Because it is the Name of God. It is serious to call You God. I do not know why I am saying this. I think it is because I want You to know I do not use Your Name without being a serious person. Some people are not serious when they use Your Name. They say it without seriousness. Sometimes they say it as a swear word. When they do this they have no respect for You. Pastor Nate says respect for You is called reverence. I have reverence. People should do reverence when they use Your Name. God, You are a serious person. This is why I trust You.

So then I walked to the church, but I got lost. And this is a bad feeling. I am always getting lost. I never know I am lost until I am. This is scary for me. When Emily drove away, I walked for a little while and listened to my Blue Day mixtape. I got to a street corner and I did not know where I was. I did not remember this street and I did not remember if I had been on this street before. I got my Polaroid photos out of my bag because I needed to see if I had photos of the street I was on. But I did not have Polaroid photos of this street. God, I keep my Polaroid photos with me because I have taken many photos of Morning, New York ever since I became not smart. When I am lost I always check my photos to see if one of them is the same as where I am. Sometimes they are and also sometimes they are not. If the photo is the same, then I find myself. If the photo is not the same, I have lost myself. Then I am afraid. Sometimes I am afraid I will never be found. When I do not find myself, the first thing I do is pray to You and I just do what You say. So that is what I did after Emily drove away because I was lost and could not find myself. I prayed to You, God, and I said, God I am lost and I am afraid. The bad voices came back and said bad things when I was praying and I did not like it, but I prayed anyway. Then You spoke to me. I did not hear words in my head, but I did in my heart and my stomach. Emily says sometimes God speaks to your gut. She means stomach. God, You spoke to my gut. You made me remember a long time ago, the first time I got lost after I became not smart, and I was afraid then too, and I prayed to You then too, and You said go to the cornfield at the end of town and I did, and then I could see everything and also I could go anywhere. Today I did that. I walked outside of town and it took fifty-seven minutes and I know because I looked at my watch. When I got to the cornfield I looked back and I saw the entire whole town, but in my head. It was like You picked me up and showed me. I saw the old movie theater that is closed, I saw Stegman's Grocery Store and Market Street, and our church. The church is where I had to go and that is where I went. It was easy. I know I will get lost again, but I am not afraid.

I have been lost many times in life.

But when I get lost You always find me.

You always bring me where I need to be.

I got to the church, but I was late. Pastor Nate told me I was an hour late when I got there. I told him I was sorry. He asked me where I went. So I told him I got lost but then I got found. He laughed and told me there was a lot going on in what I said. But I did not understand. I thought about this because the Bible says, Be quick to listen and slow to speak. This verse is from James 1:19. So I did that. But I still did not understand. How can a person can see words and see a lot going on in words? I do not see anything when people talk, I just hear words. I thought for so long that Pastor Nate asked me what was wrong.

I told him I did not understand because you cannot see words I say so how can you see a lot going on in words that I said? Pastor Nate laughed again and shook his head and told me to forget it, and he told me we still had lots of time. And I knew You made this happen because You are always on time, God, especially in church. So we went into the church.

I feel good inside church.

Church is where You are, but You are in me too. My church is called Morning Church. I come to Morning Church every Blue Day and every Sunday. There are other churches in Morning, but this church is mine. Many people come to Morning Church. Emily says lots of people go to church but do not accept Jesus Christ as their Lord and Savior. That means they do not listen for Your Voice, and they do not do what You say, and they do not think You talk to them or that You are in control of things. But You are in control of things. Emily says lots of people do not like going to church because sometimes Pastors yell at them and then people think they are bad. That does not make any truth to me. If a person is in trouble they should talk to You and You will get them out of trouble. Emily said that some people hate church. This makes no truth either. The Bible says, As for God, His way is Perfect. This is from Psalm 18:30. I do not know why someone would not want to learn the perfect thing. This makes me want to read my Bible and go to church more because if I do things Your Way, then I am doing it perfect. I am happy to do things perfect and be in the house of God.

I also like the music.

I also like the church people.

I also like Pastor Nate.

Pastor Nate teaches me things every Blue Day. Ira and Ernie always come to the church too. But Ira and Ernie only come one Blue Day a week, which is Thursday. But not today. Today is Tuesday. But it is still a Blue Day. Nora is always at church too. Nora is always practicing with the choir and that is what she was doing when I got there. People were doing Bible study so Pastor Nate brought me to the Sunday School room, but it is not Sunday. This is where we went and I sat in a chair at the table and then Pastor Nate sat across from me. He asked me about my day. I told him again how I was lost but I got found and how You found me. He laughed again, but I did not understand why he laughed. He smiles and laughs when he teaches me things and it is fun.

This is why Pastor Nate is my friend.

A friend is someone you can talk to.

God, You are my friend too.

It is a good feeling to talk to someone. I tell him things that I cannot tell anyone else except You. Today, I wanted to tell him about the voices when I prayed, but I also did not want to tell him. I told him before when it happened and that is why he said to write it down. But now it happens a lot. Sometimes I do not like telling him things because I am afraid he will not understand. But he always understands, so I do not know why I am afraid. When he stopped laughing it got quiet and we did not talk and it made me feel weird and I wanted to leave.

He said, So what else happened today?

I did not look at him. I did not feel good. My face hurt. My eyes hurt. Then Pastor Nate asked me why I was crying. I said, I did not know I was crying but I suppose I am crying so then I am.

But I pulled my hat down because I did not want him to see me cry because someone told me one time that it is a bad thing if people see you cry, but I also do not remember who said this so I do not know if it is a truth. Then he asked me what was wrong. I told him that I heard the voices when I prayed and he said it was okay. And I said it is not okay.

He said, Tell me what the voices say.

I told him I will not say.

He asked me why.

I told him, Because I do not want to go to hell.

He said, You think you're going to hell?

I told him I cannot say what the voices say or I will die here first and then die second for forever because that is what hell is. He was quiet for a little bit and I stopped crying which was not easy because I did not know I was crying in the first place, but my face was hard and my eyes were wet.

Pastor Nate said, You're saved, you're not going to hell. When you die, you'll be with Christ because He's the one who saved you and He doesn't let go.

I did not talk.

Pastor Nate said, Do you know the verse, This sickness is not unto death? Jesus says it when He's told that Lazarus is sick, and He tells Martha and her sister that this sickness will not end in death. You have a sickness, but it will not lead to death. Those voices are not from you, and they are certainly not from God. You have nothing to fear.

I nodded my head but I did not talk.

Then Pastor Nate and me prayed and asked for the voices to go away forever. It was good. When Pastor Nate prays it is not weird. He just says the things that need to be said to You. I have heard some people pray and sometimes it feels like a false and I do not like it. But then we finished praying. Pastor Nate looked at me, and You spoke to me, and I remembered a verse from the Bible, and this is that verse. For our struggle is not against flesh and blood, but against the rulers, against the authorities, against the powers of this dark world and against the spiritual forces of evil in the heavenly realms. This verse is from Ephesians 6:12. I told this to Pastor Nate, and this verse gave me even more hope. And also I knew You were speaking to me. Also my stomach was warm and my face was warm and my eyes were warm and I felt good.

Pastor Nate said, Why are you crying again, Todd?

I said, I did not know I was crying but I suppose I am but I am not sad this time because God still loves me and keeps me safe.

I knew this was a truth.

This gave me more hope.

This is a good feeling.

I kept feeling good when I left the church.

But I did not go home.

I went to see Izzy.

On Blue Days I always go see Izzy. I know the way. But I got lost again, and then I found myself again. The place I found myself was on a street that made me really afraid. It was dark. The wind was blowing hard and the sky had dark clouds, and the trees shook, but it did not rain. It got cold for a second but then it was warm near me and I think You did that and I said God, thank You for making it warm near me because this is scary and weird. The street I was on was called Morgan Street. And that is when I lost myself. So I opened my backpack and got my photos. I found a photo of Morgan Street, and this was the street I was on. When I saw this photo I knew where I was. Morgan Street goes all the way up a hill, and if you go all the way up the hill, Morning Home is there behind a lot of pine trees with a big, black, old rusty gate at the top of the hill. This is where I went, and it made me afraid because the sky had dark clouds the whole way and the trees kept shaking and it did this all the way up the hill. The sky got darker when I got to Morning Home. I was afraid, but I remembered what You said, God. You said, Have I not commanded you? Be strong and courageous. Do not be afraid, do not be discouraged, for the Lord Your God is with you wherever you go. This is in Joshua 1:9. I remembered this and decided to not be afraid, even though I sort of was afraid.

Emily says this is called being brave.

Being brave is doing a thing when you are afraid. I am brave whenever I go to Morning Home. I am brave because Morning Home is weird and makes people afraid. Everything is old and scary and there is a button that you have to press at the gate to say your name. I pressed this button and a voice came out of the speaker next to the button. The voice told me to state my name.

I said my name is Todd.

The voice said, What's your last name, Todd, I tell you every time.

So I said, My name is Todd Carpenter, who are you?

The voice said, You know who this is, dude. I talk to you every Tuesday and Thursday. We've been doing this for like ten years.

But I did not remember this so I did not know who this was.

I said, I am sorry, I forgot who you are.

The voice made a noise and said a bad word that I did not hear.

I said, I did not hear you.

The voice in the speaker yelled, Who are you here for, Todd?

I thought about this. The voice said he talks to me every Tuesday and Thursday, so if that is a truth I do not know why he asked me all these questions.

The voice said, You there or what, dude?

I said, If you know me why are you asking me so many questions?

The voice said, I have to do this for the book, just give me the answers.

I said, The answers to what?

Then the voice swore many times and he said all the bad ones in a row.

He said, Are you just messing with me, man?

But he did not say the word, Messing. He used another word, and it was a swear word, and it the worst one there is so I cannot write it. Also the Bible says, Do not let any unwholesome talk come out of your mouth. This is from Ephesians 4:29. So I cannot write what he said, but it was bad.

Then he said, Dude, are you just messing with me?

I said, No, sir.

He said, Who do you want to see, Todd?

I said, I am here to see Izzy.

The voice said, You mean, Isabel Eaton?

I said, Yes, but she likes to be called Izzy.

The voice said, Shut up, Todd.

I did not like that. I wanted to say a bad word back, but I did not do that. Then there was a loud buzz and the gate opened slow and I walked in. Then I forgot I was angry because then I got afraid again. But I was still being brave. I decided to have even more braveness. The more I am afraid, the more I have to be brave. I had a lot of braveness. I also had sadness.

But I did not know why.

I had madness too.

But I also did not know why.

But I still had braveness. That is because this place is scary. When I enter the gate, I always have to walk on a sidewalk next to a road with pine trees on the side and forest behind them until I get to the building and it is always scary. The forest is dark and goes on for a long, long time. This is scary too, but Jesus Christ is in my heart and spirit so I am okay. And the sidewalk curves and goes in a circle and then you get to the building. I do not like the building because it looks like a scary castle from a long time ago. It is big with many rooms and windows, but all of the windows have bars on them. I still had madness, but now I knew why. People are trapped here. I do not think it is right. Sometimes I pray to be someone else. Sometimes I pray to be smart and a warrior person like a knight in King Arthur times. That way I could save the sad people. Sometimes I pray to have a stronger body and a stronger heart. My heart is not that strong. My heart is sad a lot. My heart is sad now because people have to be here.

I am sad that Izzy lives here.

I never want to go inside.

But I always go inside.

It was dark. I did not like it. A light is always flickering above the door where I enter, and it goes bzz and bzz and it was always this way. It gave me madness, but I did not do or say anything because Pastor Nate says madness is a choice and I want to always choose goodness. But I do not like this place because it is bad and because of the person who sits behind the desk.

That person said, Sign here, dummy.

It is the person who opened the gate. The name of this person is Morton Marlowe. I do not like him. He is chubby and stares at Izzy. He thinks bad things about her but I do not know what he thinks. He did it one time and I wanted to hit him, but I did not because I know You will punish him. And also maybe he will turn into a good person so I have prayed for him to be a good person. But he is not good now, so I do not like him now. Every time I am here he points to a hallway and calls me dummy and tells me to go that way. But I never yell at him. I want to yell at him, and tell him he is a dummy and he is fat, but I never do. I do not because he is still Your Creation. I know You will deal with him. So I go and the hallway lights above me are bright and they make me close my eyes and also they go off and on and *bzz* and *bzz* and are yellow and white. And also it is still dark even with the lights. It is dark always here. I hate darkness. But it is light in the television room so that is good. And that is where Izzy is.

Sometimes Izzy does not look pretty.

But she is still pretty even when she is not.

Izzy is the prettiest girl in the entire whole world.

It is not right that Izzy is alone. She is always in the television room with other people, but she is alone. Sometimes she reads books and sometimes she listens to music and sometimes I give her my mixtapes so she can listen to my music too. Sometimes she plays chess with another person. Sometimes she is happy. Sometimes she is sad. Sometimes she reads to me *The Once and Future King* by a person named T.H. White. Other times she reads to me *Peter Pan* by a person named J.M. Barrie. Sometimes she talks to me and I never say anything. Sometimes only I talk and she does not say anything. Sometimes she does none of this. Sometimes she says nothing to me and stares. This is what she did today. When Izzy says nothing and stares, it is because she is sad in her heart.

When I saw her I said, Hi, Izzy.

Izzy did not look at me. She did not say anything at all. She only stared. Her hair was messy too. She was wearing jeans and a gray sweater that I thought was a blanket, but it was not, because it had sleeves.

I said to Izzy, I thought that was a blanket but it has sleeves.

I do not like when she stares like this. It is sad when Izzy is sad. When she is this way she likes it when you hold her hand, so I did. Sometimes she cries when I do this. I held her hand for one hour and fifteen minutes and she did not speak, but it was okay. She only stared. Then it was time to leave so I got my Luke Skywalker toy from my backpack. The last time I was here I promised Izzy I would bring it and the only promise I ever broke was the one I promised Emily about coming to see Izzy so I cannot break any more promises.

I said, Here is my Luke Skywalker toy I promised you.

That is when she spoke.

She said, Todd, don't go.

I said, Okay, Izzy.

So I sat back down. She gave me her hand so I held her hand for many more minutes. It was for forty-nine minutes. That is when I told Izzy I had to go. She did not say anything. It is okay. I opened her hand and I put the toy in her hand. She did not talk. I closed her hand.

I said, You can give it back to me later.

I stood up to leave and I left. I did not want to, God. But I did. I am glad she has my Luke Skywalker toy. I do not want her to be alone.

I was alone too.

But I was not alone because You are with me.

When I am lost, I feel alone, but I know I am not.

I was on a street and I was lost, because I was praying. I was praying for a long time. I was thinking about Izzy and why she is sad always. I do not know why this is. I prayed for Izzy while I walked. I prayed in my mind, but it was bad because the voices returned. So I prayed in whispers, but the voices came back again. So I prayed in regular talk, and this time I did it out loud, and I prayed so I heard me, and so the evil voices heard me too. I hate the evil voices. God, they confuse me. I hate them all. So I prayed real loud for a long time. But I was also not thinking about where I was. When I was done praying, I was lost.

It was dark all over.

I was under a streetlight.

The light was shining around me.

Everything was quiet. It was cold, and the wind was cold. The wind was blowing hard and the wind was mean wind. The wind pushed my face and it made my head turn. My head turned and I saw the movie theater. It was empty with boards on the doors. I remembered this place. This was the old movie theater that me and Izzy used to go to when I was smart. Izzy also brought me here after I turned not smart and Emily did too. But God, then we could not come here anymore and I remember we had to go to the other movie theater at the mall because this place closed. We used to see many movies here and I remembered them all when I stood there. But the wind was pushing me around and it was scaring me, God. It was pushing me away from the movie theater and the voices were telling me to run far away and be afraid. The wind was telling to go home.

God, the wind was scary. But there was a light at the door. There was a bright light inside the theater. It was strong, so strong it burned the boards. I know because I saw between the boards on the windows because I put my face to it and the boards were hot. God, this is when You talked. You always talk to me, but this is when You really talked to me, God. You talked in my heart and head. You told me to go in and said the wind cannot hurt me. But the wind was speaking too and it was telling me not to go inside. And I was afraid. So I did not go inside.

I am sorry, God.

I knew it was You.

But also I was afraid it was not You.

I was afraid it was something else. I am dumb, but I am not stupid. Pastor Nate says always double check to make sure I am hearing God correct. Because there are bad things out there like demons. Demons are all liars. And also it was late and I am always home watching a movie before Emily gets home and if I am not there she will be mad. God, I did not go in the theater, but only because I need to double check with You. I prayed that You were not mad with me. I knew You were not mad, but I still prayed anyway. The wind was blowing harder, and it was a mean and bad wind. It moved me away from the movie theater. The light inside got bigger and it was coming out of the boards. It was warm and my face and eyes were warm and I said, God I am afraid. And my eyes hurt and I cried, but I did not know I was crying until I was. The light touched my skin. The light was hot, but it did not burn me. The wind was strong but it did not hurt me. The wind got louder, and the light got brighter. There was screaming in the wind. The wind said terrible things I cannot say but I will tell You it was all swear words and also it said I was dumb. The wind got louder, but the light got brighter. And the light blew up and it was all bright everywhere and so bright I could not see. It was not bright white like in movies. And it was not sunlight either. It was Truth Light. It was so light that I could not see for a long time and I was not afraid. And then everything was quiet.

Then the storm was over.

I opened my eyes and I could see.

I was not lost anymore.

So I ran home, and got home. But it was not Home Home yet. It is not Home Home until the lights are on and the television is on and Emily is home. Even when it is Home Home, it is not Truth Home, and will never be in this life. Truth Home is Heaven, and that will be someday. But Emily was not home and she would be home soon. I turned on the lights and the television. When Emily comes home I am always already watching a movie. But I was not watching a movie yet. If I was not watching a movie, Emily would know I was out and she would know I went to see Izzy because Emily is smart. She would be mad. I did not want Emily to be mad because madness is not good for her. I hooked up the VCR and I put in Star Wars. Emily does not like the VCR. She does not like my tape player and does not like my tapes. She says the VCR is twenty years old and says my tape player is thirty years old. She hates them. She gets mad because sometimes the VCR and my tape player break and then it takes a long time to get it fixed. She says nobody has a VCR anymore and nobody uses a tape player anymore. But I do. I like to watch movies on a VCR. I like to listen to music on my mixtapes. To me it is a truth. Emily watches television and movies too, but you cannot hold any of them. They are just there inside the television. To me that is a big false. It is not real. Real is a truth. A truth is a right. A right is never a wrong. That is why it is hard to lie and you do not feel good when you lie. Because it is very bad. I do not lie. I never lie except sometimes, but I always feel bad after and apologize to You, God. But I lied to Emily when she got home. When Emily got home I finished hooking up the VCR and pressed play. She walked in the house at the exact same second I pressed play. Emily did not know.

She said, When did you get home?

I said, I got home a while ago.

But this was not a truth. This was a lie, and in my mind I told You I was sorry for lying. And then she asked if I was hungry and I told her yes, because I was hungry. She made macaroni and cheese because I like it. We ate dinner and watched Star Wars. We were both happy. Now it was Home Home.

Sometimes Home Home is in the middle of the day.

Sometimes Home Home is in the morning.

Sometimes Home Home is at night.

Lots of times when I am home and it is Home Home, I want to tell Emily things, but I do not because I cannot. I wanted to tell her about my day, but I did not. Then the movie ended. So I went to the kitchen to drink water. I saw a star in the sky. That is because I can look at the sky through the window above the sink. I went outside to look at the sky and the screen door made a loud creak noise because it always does. This is how Emily knew I was outside.

So Emily came out and said, Todd, what are you doing?

And I was hoping. I wanted to say this to Emily but I do not know how. So I said, I am not doing anything. She did not say anything and she turned around and went back inside. I would like tell her I was hoping, but she just would not understand what I want to say. I would like to tell her how I hope for things. I hope for many things, God. I hope for Emily. I hope she knows I know it is hard to take care of me. I hope I get smarter so she does not have to do this anymore. I hope to tell her so many things. I hope one day I can.

Hoping is my favorite thing.

But hoping without God is not hope.

So I always hope with You, God.

Sometimes I hope that Emily would talk to me and I would be able to understand her and that she would be able to understand me. But things are always ununderstandable between us. One thing I hope for is for it to be like the before times and before I was dumb.

The before times were good.

I remember one time I was looking at the stars the way I am now and this was the before times when I was smart. Emily came out and she held my hand, and then she asked me what I was thinking about and I said I am thinking about the purpose of things, and she smiled at me and kissed my forehead. Then I looked at Emily and I asked her what my purpose was, and she smiled at me and she said, It will find you, that's life. And then we stayed that way for a long, long while and it was good. Sometimes life is good. Sometimes life is not so good. But You are good always, God. So sometimes I like to look out at the sky and hope good things, because I know You are looking at me hoping good things. You know my hopes and then it is me and You and we are hoping good things together.

I know You have good plans for me because it says so in the Bible. That is why I am hoping now. When I look at the stars I know it is a truth. Because You made stars. Sometimes I wonder if You made stars just for us. Sometimes when I look at the stars, I think they are hopes that belong to others. I think maybe when someone has a new hope, You and the Angels make a star. I do not know if this is a truth, but it is not a false. A truth is that You made stars. This is to remind others You are real and You are the real hope for all people. It says in the Bible, Light shines in the darkness and the darkness has not overcome it. This is from John 1:5. Stars shine in darkness, and that is like You. I do not know how people cannot hope. If someone wants to know You are real, they just need to look up. But people hate when I say things like this because they do not want hope.

 Emily had a boyfriend once, and he did not have hope. His name was Jacob. He did not believe Jesus Christ was Your Son. He was not happy. He was always mad. He wore black jeans and red flannel shirts and shoes not sneakers. He was skinny and wore glasses. Emily said he was a drug addict. Emily and him were going to get married and then did not. He was not nice. He was mean. He said mean things and said them meanly. One time he said that stars are just gas, and space is just nothingness. And then I said, God made all the stars so space is full of somethingness not nothingness. I also said that was a truth, but he laughed at me and shook his head and called me dumb and told me the reason I was dumb was because of God. Then I had madness. I yelled at him and I pushed him. Emily was not there so she does not know so it is okay and I will never tell her. And I said to him, It is sad when people have no hope in God because then they have no hope at all and it is sad when they have no hope in Jesus Christ because then they truly have no hope at all. He said there is no God. He said he felt sad for me. I said nothing, but my madness went away and I had sadness for him. I do not care anymore about it because I gave him forgiveness from in my heart because he is stupid and sucks. Instead, I have hope for him. I hope now there is a star for him.

 And I hope there is a star for me.

 You have enough stars for everyone.

 That is life.

Eleven

THE CHRONICLES OF EMILY PART II

God, I did a wrong thing.

I have read Part Two.

I did not like it.

This is because Part Two was sad and made me remember the truth I do not like. Emily does not know the truth I do not like. Nobody knows but You. I am glad for that because nobody would like me if they knew and then Emily would leave me forever. I will never ever tell anyone the truth for as long as I live. I will die with it. I hate that truth because it is my fault.

I also did not like her friends in Part Two.

They are not her friends anymore.

Emily did not have good friends.

Her friends were mean to her. Emily wrote all of this in her book. But I also know this because I saw her friends be mean to her. Also her friends were mean to me too. I do not know why. They were not good. They were pretty in their faces, but not in their hearts. Their hearts were gross. It is why they were mean. I feel bad for people with gross hearts. They do not know their hearts are gross. If they knew, they would go to Jesus Christ to get good hearts. I know this because in the Bible it says this in a verse. This is that verse. And I will give you a new heart, and I will put a new spirit in you. I will take out your stony, stubborn heart and give you a tender, responsive heart. And I will put my Spirit in you so that you will follow my decrees and be careful to obey my regulations.

And this verse is from Ezekiel 36:26. And also, this is a promise. So if a person knows they have a gross heart, they should go to You to get a good, new pretty heart. But her friends had gross, cold hearts and they were mean to Emily and they were mean to me. This is in her book. Some things I remember because I was there, and some things I do not because I was not there. One thing I know is that Jacob was mean to Emily. I was not there, but I saw it in many pictures. Jacob has a gross heart too. I know because I read how Jacob was mean, but I never saw it. One thing that I do not remember is when Emily and Jacob screamed at each other this one time. I was not there, but I know because I read it in The Chronicles of Emily Carpenter, Part Two. She drew many pictures and wrote many words. Some words I knew and some words I did not. The pictures were Emily and Jacob screaming. Many words were bad. But some were not bad. In the pictures she found underwear at his house and it was not hers. She said she hated Jacob. She called him a cheater and other bad words I am not allowed to say. Jacob called her names. He is a bad person. In the pictures he said she was a waste of talent because she did not run away to New York City with him and she would never be anything and be stuck here in town forever. Then she said she had to take care of me and it is why she became a nurse and did not go. Then she said she hated being a nurse. This makes me sad because it is my fault. If I was not here Emily would not have to be a nurse and hate her life. But she does hate her life. If Emily did not hate her life then she could be happy with Jacob, but she is not happy even a little. But I am glad they yelled at each other. It is better for Emily to be not happy now, but happy later. If she were happy now then she would be not happy later. Because Jacob sucks. That is because he hurt Emily and I love her. Another reason I do not like Jacob is because I know how he hurt Emily, but Emily does not know this. It is a thing I remember because I was there. I know because I wrote it down in the Calendar of Todd. This was on a Saturday. It was July Fourth, Nineteen Ninety-Eight at One Twenty-One in the afternoon. I was in the living room by myself. I was watching The Empire Strikes Back and I was happy. Emily came home with her friends. Her friends were named Sandra and Becky. Sandra had long red hair and Becky had short blonde hair. Sandra and Becky were pretty in their faces but they were gross and cold in their hearts. Sandra is like the Dark Phoenix in X-Men because in X-Men, the Dark Phoenix is when Jean Grey gets mean and she is a horrible person. And Becky is like Emma Frost in X-Men because in X-Men, Emma Frost has ice powers and she is evil and has a cold heart, but also she is really pretty. They are bad in X-Men, and Sandra and Becky are bad in real life. And they came into the living room on Saturday July Fourth, Nineteen Ninety-Eight at One Twenty-One and their hair was all wet because they were swimming and then they were going back outside somewhere. I know this because they told me. Emily said she had to change and then she went to her room and Sandra and Becky stayed in the living room with me. Sandra and Becky were wearing not enough clothes. They were wearing swim suits, but the swim suits were too small for their bodies. It made me feel weird. Also, I did not think this was right because a person is supposed to cover themselves and the parts they were supposed to cover were not covered good and I could see things. I did not want to look at them. So I did not look at them and I watched the movie instead and I just wanted them to leave so I could watch the movie, but they stayed. It was my favorite part when Yoda is teaching Luke to learn. Then Sandra talked to Becky.

Sandra said, Guess who came over last night?

Becky said, Shut up, like, I know, but don't say.

Sandra said, Why not?

Becky said, Todd is here.

Sandra said, He's retarded.

Becky said, Stop it, he's going to hear and tell Emily.

Sandra said, Hey, retard, can you hear me? See, he's an idiot.

But I did hear her, and I wanted to kick her but I did not and I did not say anything to her or look at her and I only watched my movie so I was good. But then Sandra came over to me and put her face close to mine and she whispered loud and she told me she had sex last night. I wanted to leave but I did not know where to go. I did not feel good and I tried to leave but could not and said something more but I do not remember. Then my stomach hurt and I opened my mouth. I made a gross noise and my stomach hurt and was warm and something came out of my nose and mouth and this is when I threw up on Sandra.

I felt good.

But Sandra and Becky screamed. Then Emily ran out of her room and Sandra and Emily yelled at each other. Sandra said it was my fault. Emily said it was not my fault. Sandra called me a retard. Emily said I was seven and not retarded. Emily said that Sandra must have done something to make me sick. And that is a truth, but I do not know what Sandra did. Emily asked me what Sandra did and I said I did not know because I did not know what she did so I was not lying. But Emily said she knew what Sandra did. Then Emily punched Sandra in her face with her fist and Sandra and Becky left. Then I cried and Emily hugged me and told me that I was not sick and it was okay.

That is why I did not like her friends.

Her friends had gross hearts. I did not like that Sandra called me an idiot and retard because that was wrong. I am not a retard. I am dumb. That is because of my brain when I died but came back. But I am also an idiot because I am dumb. It is a truth, but it is a mean truth. Sometimes a mean truth does not need to be said over again. Just because I am dumb does not mean someone needs to keep telling me I am dumb. It is mean. And only mean people do that. They should get punished bad. I did not want to throw up on Sandra, but I am glad I did. Because I think she saw how gross and cold her heart was. I think it is why You made me throw up on her. Sometimes a girl can be pretty in her face but gross and cold in her heart and then her face is just a stupid false.

That is why I do not like The Chronicles of Emily, Part Two.

Because Emily had bad friends.

And of the truth I do not like.

But I will not say that truth. The truth I do not like is a sin. Nobody knows what happened even though they know. But they do not know everything. God, only me and You know. I know You have forgiven me. But I have still not forgiven myself. I still feel bad about the truth I do not like. That is because I remembered the truth when I read The Chronicles of Emily Carpenter, Part Two. Sometimes I am punished because I have to remember the truth I do not like. But this is justice. I should be punished. I am sorry, God.

Please forgive me.

Twelve

THE PRISONERS OF MORNING HOME

God, You are a hero.

I want to be a hero too.

Heroes set people free.

God, You are also cool. That is what cool people do. That is also what they do in the movies. I think the movies got this from You. You say in the Bible, So if the Son sets you free, you will be free indeed. This is from John 8:36. That is what I am going to do too. I am going to do it for my friends. I will set them free. I do not know when. But I will do this because they are prisoners at Morning Home. I will free them. I will be like You, God. I am going to be cool about it too.

It will be good.

But I did not free them today. Today was a Blue Day Thursday. And I could not do it today because I did not know what to do. Instead I was talking with Ernie and Ira in the television room. This is what we do when I am there. Sometimes we do not talk at all and just watch television. Sometimes we watch television and talk. And when we talk, the king of the television room yells at us. He is not a real king, he just calls himself a king, so I will not capitalize his name. But he says he is the king of the television room. I asked Ira why the king of the television room wears a sheet on his back and a weird hat. Ira said it is because the king of the television room is a total sociopath so we have got to be cool. He said the sheet is a cape and the hat is a fedora. And do not call the sheet a sheet or the hat a hat. If we call the sheet a sheet or the hat a hat, the king of the television room will get angry and scream and then it will be bad. Then Ernie and Ira cannot watch what they want to watch because the King controls the television. I told them this is not fair. Ira said it is easier this way. So today we said hello to the King. Once we did that, the King was in a nice mood and he let us watch whatever we wanted to watch. Ernie wanted to watch He-Man so that is what we watched. It was good. But it was not fair. Because Ernie and Ira should not have to fear another person when they want to watch He-Man. This is why they are prisoners. They are also prisoners because they do what Morton says. Morton is the chubby, gross person who stares at Izzy. He is mean to my friends. He yells at Ernie and Ira. I know this because Ernie and Ira told me. I have not seen it. That is because they say Morton only does it when there are no visitors. I did not like this. I told Ernie and Ira to tell Pastor Nate but Ira said nobody would believe them. Ernie said one time he did not want to take the pills anymore because they make him sleepy. So Ernie told Morton that he would not take the pills anymore, and Morton hit Ernie in the face. Then Ernie told Morton he would take the pills, but Ernie is smart and he hides the pills in his mouth. Morton does not hit Ira, but he does other bad things to him. If Ira reads late at night, Morton takes away his books. I did not like this at all. I hate this. Because my friends are prisoners. This is why I will free them someday.

 It will be a good feeling.

 Then they can go anywhere. But I do not know where. They will go to a new world. Maybe it will be Heaven. I do not want them to die, God. I just want them to be free. Heaven is the only place we will be free. Right now we are on Earth and we are free because Jesus set us free, but we are here. That is why I am ready for Jesus to come back, then we will be Truth Free and go to Heaven. Because when Jesus comes back it will not be like the first time You were here. It will be different. Pastor Nate says nobody really knows what it will be like, but I read the Bible, so I know things. The Bible says Jesus Christ is coming back on a white horse with fire in His Eyes. It says that He and the Angels will fight the devil and demons and Jesus will kill them. That is cool too. It is also scary. I do not want to be here on Earth when it happens. I want to be with You in Heaven. I do not know when this will be. But until then, I want Ernie and Ira to be free.

I want this for Izzy too.

She is also a prisoner.

Izzy needs freedom.

She wants to go far away. She told me this once. She tells me this a lot. It is sad. One time when she first got to Morning Home, I asked her why she was here and she cried a lot. Sometimes when I come to see Izzy, she cries the entire whole time. I stay there and hug her. The very first time Izzy cried to me was on Thursday, October Fifth, Two Thousand and Six. I know this because I wrote it in the Calendar of Todd. Izzy cried to me before then lots of times too. But that was the first time she cried to me at Morning Home. She cried that day for a long time. I went to see her at Morning Home and she cried to me and she said she did not deserve this. She said it was unfair and that she would get them back. I asked who she would get back. She said never mind. She said she would tell me one day. But I did not ask her again to tell me. Izzy never told me. She cried many times after, but I did not write them in the Calendar of Todd. Every time Izzy cries she always says it is unfair. I have hugged Izzy many times. She is sad. She is a prisoner too. It is why I want to free her.

I would do anything for Izzy. This is because I love her. Love is the best thing. Izzy loves me too. She did not cry when I saw her this time. She came into the television room and she ruffled my hair because that is what Izzy does sometimes but not every time. We hugged. And that is because I hug my friends. I said her name and the king of the television room got mad. He made the shushing noise. Izzy held my hand and she brought me to the back of the room. Ernie and Ira stayed up front and kept watching He-Man. I asked Izzy if she was feeling better. She was. She said she was sorry she was sad the other day. Morton made her take the pills. She says the pills make her sleepy and dumb. She did not take them today. She is good today. We sat down at a table and I told Izzy how I was writing a book to God. She liked that. She asked me what it was about and I said it is about my life and the things I do in the daytime and nighttime too if it is night. Izzy said she has a book like that, but it was not to God. She said it was the story of her life. I told Izzy that I would like to read the story of her life. She said no because it was only for her. Then I said, Okay.

She also said I could not read it because they took it from her a few days ago. Sometimes they give it back, but she does not think she will get it back this time. I asked her who took her book. She said it was Morton. She said that he has done this before. She said that sometimes he gives it back to her, but this time she hit him and she does not think she will get it back ever again. I told her that was not fair. Izzy said that many things in life are unfair. God, I decided I would do something good for Izzy. I decided to get her book back. I did not tell Izzy I would do this because I might get caught. I prayed for Your Help too. I know You say not to steal but this is a good thing so I am going to do it. That is because I am doing a Truth so I think it is okay. And I am doing this for my friend Izzy. Because real love is when you sacrifice for your friends. I know this is right because it is in the Bible and says this in a verse. Here is that verse. There is no greater love than to lay down one's life for one's friends. That is good. That verse is from John 15:13. That is what You did. That is what heroes do.

I want to be a hero for Izzy and Ernie and Ira.

A hero fights for his friends.

This is a hero.

Thirteen
PLANET IZZY

God, I did a bad thing.

I stole something.

But I did it for a truth.

I got Izzy her book back. I stole it from Morton the fat man. I did it yesterday. Yesterday was Blue Day Thursday. Today is Red Day Friday. I did it when I left Morning Home. I said goodbye to Ernie and Ira and Izzy. Then I walked to the front door and Morton was there. And I saw the book on his desk. He was not looking at it. He was on the phone and yelling a lot. I was not sure if it was the book, but I thought it was because it had flowers. It was a girl book. Morton was not looking at me. His head was turned the other way. So I reached over the counter. That is when I took the book and I hid it under my shirt and I ran and ran and ran away fast out the door.

I won.

God, the Bible says do not steal. But what if someone steals something from someone I love and then I steal it back because I want to do good and justice? Because Izzy could not get the book back, but I could. Is it wrong? I do not know. I was sure, but now I am not sure. God, I am confused. That is why I pray now and ask for forgiveness for stealing it if I did a sin. I am sorry.

God, I also did a second bad thing.

I am sorry for what I did.

I am going to confess it now.

I read the book. Yesterday on Blue Day Thursday, Izzy said to me her book was only for her. But I did not listen. I read her book after I stole it. It is called Planet Izzy. That is what she named it. It is sad. God, she wrote a big truth in her book. A bad thing that happened to her. She wrote in her book called Planet Izzy that her grandpa died when she was eighteen years old and left her lots of money. I do not know the amount because I did not understand the number. She wrote down the numbers. It was many. There were Zeroes, Nines, and Twos and Sevens and Fives. I did not understand. But I counted the numbers. There were eight numbers. I did not know so I went to ask Emily. But I did not tell her why. I wrote the number on another piece of paper and I asked Emily what it was. She said it was twelve million, nine hundred thousand, seven hundred and fourteen. Emily asked me what it was for and I told her it was for nothing. God, that is a lot of money that Izzy has now. But then, Izzy wrote that her parents got mad. Her parents tried to take it. She wrote that her and her parents got in a big fight and they told Izzy she did not deserve the money and her parents got lawyers and tried to take the money from her and they put her in Morning Home. It was unfair. But Izzy is smart. She wrote that she hid the money in a secret bank account and only she knows. She wrote that this bank account will make even more money. She wrote that right now the money is more money and she wrote numbers I did not understand. So I wrote the numbers on another piece of paper and I asked Emily what it meant. Emily said the number was twenty-four million, five hundred and fifty-one, and twenty-eight. But Izzy wrote that she is stuck. Izzy wrote that they keep her prisoner. They watch her. Morton the fat man always watches her and he watches grossly. She wrote that she cannot escape and that she is the wealthiest prisoner alive. She wrote she would rather die than give her parents the money because they would spend it. Izzy wants to do something big with it. She wrote that she would open new schools and buy Morning Home and take care of the people there forever and do what God wants her to do. But she is a prisoner. She wrote that she may never leave. She wrote she cannot tell anyone and nobody knows. But now I know. I will never tell anyone ever. I am sorry I read her book. But I think You wanted me to.

So then I am not sorry.

Fourteen

BATTLE OF THE BELIEVERS

God, I saw a yelling fight.

This was a hurt to see.

It was a battle.

Sometimes when people yell it hurts me bad. Sometimes they do not even yell at me. Sometimes I will hear someone yell at someone else and it hurts. I do not know why, but it does. It hurts in my chest and also in my face. The hurt will start in my heart and goes to my face and my eyes and sometimes I cry. That is what happened today. Today was a Red Day Friday.

Today, people yelled.

The people who yelled do not like each other.

I wish they did, but they do not.

The people are Pastor Nate and Doctor Hemming. They do not like each other even a little. But Pastor Nate does not hate Doctor Hemming and I know that because Pastor Nate told me. But Doctor Hemming hates Pastor Nate and I know that because I heard Doctor Hemming say it. Pastor Nate does not hate anyone. Pastor Nate says he only hates evil, and sin. He says Christians have to love everyone so he loves people and Doctor Hemming too. Pastor Nate says that it is an order from Jesus Christ so You have to obey it and love everyone. He says he loves Doctor Hemming, but does not like him, and those two things are different things. Pastor Nate said loving someone does not mean agreeing with someone, it means caring for them. Even enemies. Pastor Nate says caring for people means you sometimes have to fight for them. Also he says it is okay to defend yourself. He says we are not perfect, and sometimes what happens is we fight each other. That is what happened with Pastor Nate and Doctor Hemming. They yelled at each other today. I wanted to ask Doctor Hemming about it but he walked away. When Doctor Hemming walked away he said he really hated Pastor Nate. This is how I know Doctor Hemming hates Pastor Nate.

They were not happy with each other.

Nobody started it. Nobody did a wrong thing. But they did a wrong thing when it started. This is what happened. God, I went to get pizza at Lasullo Brothers Pizza. It is good pizza. I have never had pizza anywhere else. I do not want pizza anywhere else because it is the best there is. I am allowed to get pizza every Red Day Friday. That is what I did today. I went to get pizza. I always get two pizzas. One for me and one for Emily, but Emily only eats three slices. So then I get one entire pizza, plus another pizza, minus three slices. Also, I buy three slices to go. Sometimes I buy four, but today I bought three. So I am actually eating two entire whole pizzas. I know that because Emily once told me I was eating two entire whole pizzas. I like pizza a lot. It makes me feel good. Today I ate two slices of pizza at the counter at Lasullo Brothers Pizza. Then Mr. Lasullo gave me the two pizzas so I left and ate my third slice of pizza and walked outside. When I walked outside I saw Pastor Nate and I was going to yell, Hi Pastor Nate, but I did not. That is because I had pizza in my mouth. I saw him putting pieces of paper on car windshields. Then I saw someone walking fast behind him and it was Doctor Hemming and he looked mad. I was going to yell, Hi Doctor Hemming, but I did not. That is because I had pizza in my mouth. Doctor Hemming got the piece of paper off his car and read it and then he yelled at Pastor Nate. I cannot repeat what he said because he called Pastor Nate a bad word and it was the worst word of all the words. Pastor Nate yelled back.

Pastor Nate said, Calm down, psycho!

Doctor Hemming said, I don't want this crap on my car!

Pastor Nate said, It's not crap! It's a God given mission!

Doctor Hemming said, I don't want it anywhere near me!

Pastor Nate said, Well I didn't know it was your car!

Doctor Hemming said, Yes you did and that's why you did it!

Pastor Nate said, Stop it, you're being ridiculous!

Doctor Hemming said, No, you're ridiculous!

Then Pastor Nate closed his eyes and said, Listen, I'm sorry.

Doctor Hemming said, No you're not!

Pastor Nate said, Yes, I am, and I know you're in pain.

Doctor Hemming said, You'll be in pain if you don't get out of my face!

Then Pastor Nate and Doctor Hemming laughed. But Doctor Hemming stopped laughing and said, This isn't funny!

But it was.

Pastor Nate said, Come on man, stop this nonsense. Let God heal you.

Doctor Hemming smushed the paper in his hands and said, I hate you, Nate. If there's a God, why'd He take my family, and why'd He take the others?

Pastor Nate said, Don't talk to me like an unbeliever, you're a Christian.

Doctor Hemming said, Being a Christian's got nothing to do with me being angry! You started this, so you answer it!

Pastor Nate said, I can't answer it, Charlie.

Then Doctor Hemming said, You answer the question and you tell me why your war on guns that you put on flyers and stick on all our cars every Saturday is going to fix it and do anything at all, and you tell me how it's going to bring my wife, and my son, and my daughter back.

Pastor Nate said, There is no answer this side of Heaven, Charlie.

Doctor Hemming threw the paper ball at Pastor Nate and yelled loud, Your answer sucks so find a better answer!

I saw the entire whole thing, God.

I wanted to do something but I did not know what to do.

So I ran away.

Fifteen
THE DECEIVER NAMED JACOB

Today I learned about Jacob the deceiver.

I learned this at church today.

Because I went to church.

I always learn when I am at church. It was not boring. It was awesome. Some people think Church is boring. It is not. There are many things to learn. One thing I really like is when we learn about battles in the Bible. Like when You send Your Angels to fight against demons or bad guys. Another thing I like is when You come to Earth Yourself. I like this and it is cool. In the Bible, there is a part when You come to Earth with Your Angels. It is in Ezekiel. I remember it. This is cool. These are only some of the things I have learned about. Today I learned about something else. Today I learned about Jacob the deceiver. That is in Genesis. Jacob was a liar. Pastor Nate says the name Jacob means to deceive. That is why he was Jacob the deceiver. But he prayed to You and You changed him forever. You came down to Earth and You wrestled with Jacob all night. You won because You are God, but You are nice and let Jacob win. You said You would bless Jacob and You touched his hip and gave him a limp for the rest of his life. Pastor Nate says this was a reminder for Jacob so he would always remember to lean on God. Then you renamed him. The new name You gave him was Israel.

I thought that was cool.

You show that people change.

This is why Bible stories are cool.

I do not know why people think church is not cool. You get to hear lots of cool stories like this. Emily says not all churches are the same. Some are not as fun as ours. But some are. And also church is good. When I first went to church, I got to give my life to Jesus Christ so He can protect my soul. This is a good thing. I do not know why anyone would not do this. When you do this, you get lots of goodness back. When you say that Jesus Christ is Your Savior and ask Him to guide you and You trust in Him, He gives you a new heart and a new spirit and a home in Heaven and He protects you always. That is cool and good. The Bible says the most important commandment is to love God and people. Pastor Nate told me this world is broken by sin, and sometimes people do not love God or people. Sometimes people hate God, and they hate other people. That gives me madness. I get so much madness I want to do something. Sometimes I will turn on the television and see wrong things and people saying it is a right thing, and I will see people saying falses and then say they are telling a truth. But this is a false. They say they are fighting for God, but that is a false. That gives me so much madness that I want to hate, but I will not. I learned not to hate in church. I also learned that You are a God of mercy and love, but also justice. In the Bible there are many verses about how You are a God of justice. This is one of those verses which I am going to write after this sentence. Here is the verse. Yet the Lord longs to be gracious to you; therefore he will rise up to show you compassion. For the Lord is a God of justice. Blessed are all who wait for him! That is from Isaiah 30:18. God, that is who You are. I learned that in church. That is cool. So I do not know why people think church is not cool. I think it is because they do not trust. Because they have no hope. Me and Emily have hope. Me and Emily trust in You and we belong to You. When we left church today, Emily had hope. Then we got to the parking lot and she lost hope, because she saw someone she did not like at all.

Emily saw Jacob.

We both saw him. I do not like Jacob. Jacob is a deceiver. That means he is a liar. And he hurt Emily. He hurt her badly. When she sees him she loses hope. He always goes away for many years, then he comes back. Now he is back again. Jacob is a deceiver because he said he was going to marry Emily and then he did not marry her. He lied to her and made her sad. Also, he is a sneak. When he was with Emily a long time ago he was always asking me what I remembered about the day I died, and he would ask me when she was not around. But I never told him anything even though I remember what he did that day. I think he thinks that I remember, and I do, and that is why he is a dangerous deceiver. We both know that we both know but we do not say anything because we cannot be sure.

When we got to the parking lot he was at our car. Emily stopped and her face was white and sad. She was afraid. He was leaning against our car. He was trying to be cool. God, I do not like that because it is a false.

Jacob said, Hi, Em.

I said, Her name is Emily.

Jacob said, Hi, Todd. I see you haven't changed at all.

Emily said, What do you want?

He said, I wanted to say hi.

God, this is a false. If he wanted to say hi he would have called. I know this because Emily said, Liar, if you wanted to say hi you would have called. Then Emily said, Do yourself a favor, go to church and repent, it's right there.

He said, Em, I miss you.

She said, I'm seeing someone.

He said, Don't be stubborn, it looks bad on you.

She said, Stop attempting to be cool, it looks bad on you.

Then she walked away. And then Jacob did a bad false and grabbed her hand and told her not to walk away from him. Then Emily slapped him and she pushed me toward our car. Then we got in the car and Emily drove faster and faster and faster and then she started crying.

I said, Emily, why are you crying?

She said, Because he's a liar, he's abusive, and manipulative. He doesn't miss me, he just doesn't want to lose.

Emily is right. Jacob is a hurter. He is a liar. But I am a liar too except it is a lie that must be lied. I lie to protect Emily. I am not a hurter like Jacob. But I will hurt him if I have to.

I will never let him hurt Emily.

Sixteen
MEMORIES OF MY DAD

I had a memory today.

It was of my dad.

My dad is dead.

I only have one memory of my dad. I never wrote it in the Calendar of Todd. It is because I remember. I forgot many things, but I did not forget this. I wish I would forget this memory. It is not a good memory.

I remembered it today.

Today is Blue Day Tuesday.

But I remember it every day.

Today was my memory test. I went to see Doctor Hemming and he tested my memory. Doctor Hemming asked me what I remember about last week so I took out The Calendar of Todd to find what I needed to remember. He told me that is not what he meant. He said he wanted to me to remember from my memory. But I could not. Then he asked me to tell him what he told me last time I was there. But I could not remember. He said it was okay. Then he wrote on his notepad. Then he asked me if I remembered anything at all.

I said, Yes.

He said, What do you remember?

I said, I do not want to say.

He said, It's okay, Todd, you can tell me anything, no secrets here.

I said, I forgot.

But I did not forget.

I remembered.

And I lied.

He said it was okay, but it was not okay. It was not okay because I lied. The thing I remembered I have never told anyone ever. I did not feel good about lying so then I told Doctor Hemming that I lied to him.

He said, What do you mean you lied?

I said, I did remember something, but I did not want to say.

Doctor Hemming said, What did you remember, Todd?

I said, I am afraid to tell you what it is.

He said, You can tell me.

God, then I lied again. I was going to tell him, but I did not. I got my backpack and took out the picture I drew of Doctor Hemming for him for his birthday. I gave it to him and I said, Happy birthday, Doctor Hemming, this is for you. Doctor Hemming looked at it and he did not speak at first, then he did.

He said, You drew this, Todd?

I said, Yes, Doctor Hemming.

He said, Why did you do this?

Then I said, Because it was your birthday and I wanted to, so I did.

He said, You remind me of my son, Todd.

Then there was water in his eyes, God. He was sad. Doctor Hemming took his glasses off and wiped his eyes.

I said, Your son is with God now.

Doctor Hemming said, I'm not sure I believe that, Todd.

I told him that he should believe it because it is true and because God is a good God and He protects children. I was afraid when I said this. I did not know why. He smiled. I think he believed it, God.

He said, You are a gift to us all.

Then his throat made a noise and he said, Okay, back to business. I want you to remember what I am about to say. Remember this word, Todd, and the word is this. Music. Do not write it down, just remember. Now tell me, what is the word I just told you to remember?

I said, Music.

He said, Remember that. I will ask you next week what the word is.

I nodded my head and smiled.

Then he said, And if you want to tell me something, you can, anytime.

I said, Yes, Doctor Hemming.

And I wanted to say the thing I really remembered, but I did not. The thing I really remembered was bad. It would make Doctor Hemming sad.

What I remembered was the bad day.

It was the day lots of people died.

This is the day I died too.

It was the worst day of my life, God. This was also the day my dad died. I remember it all. I remember everything that happened. I remember everything because I just do. I do not need to write it down. I remember. I have never written it down and I never will. I see it always. It is stuck in my mind. I cannot get it out and it will not leave. It is like a movie that plays over and over again. It is when I saw many people get shot and killed. I have never told anyone, God. I will never tell anyone. I only told You, because You are God, and also You already know even if I did not tell You. But I remember. I remember what happened also because it is all my fault, God. They called my dad a coward. I remember that too. But he is not a coward. Everyone hates him, but I do not. I love him. He was a good dad. They should not hate him. They should hate me.

I am the coward.

Seventeen

PASTOR NATE AND HIS GUNS

God, something bad almost happened.

    A boy brought a gun to the school. It was on the news. Emily told me this. She said lots of people are mad. It happened today. Today was Blue Day Thursday. Emily said that the boy was going to shoot another boy because of a girl, but Pastor Nate stopped him. He was there because the school wanted him to talk about drugs. Pastor Nate tackled him. The news person talked to Pastor Nate, and I know because me and Emily watched him talk on TV. Pastor Nate said the boy pointed a gun at another boy and everyone ran and yelled. But the boy who almost got shot started crying, and then the boy with the gun cried too. Then Pastor Nate tackled the boy with the gun and held him. Pastor Nate said he had to do it. The news person said Pastor Nate kept the boy still by hugging him real tight so he could not move. Then Pastor Nate said he urged everyone to talk to troubled people or else this would happen again. He said to the camera not to forget the tragic events of that day twenty-six years ago. He said guns are for cops and soldiers but not civilians. Then Emily looked at me and said never to tell Pastor Nate that we have two guns. Then on the TV the news person said the boy cried and peed his pants. They asked Pastor Nate if it was true. Then Pastor Nate said that the boy did a regretful thing that he regrets deeply.

    I know what this means.

    Because I have a regret too.

    And I regret it deeply.

Eighteen

THE
NOT
FORGIVEN

God, I am glad You forgive us.

Being not forgiven is bad.

Being not forgiven hurts.

I know because I saw someone who is not forgiven. I saw her at the grocery store today. Today was Red Day Friday. Today I woke up at Five Fifteen like I wake up on All Days. I did my talking with You when I woke up and we had a good conversation and You said things. You almost always talk to me using the Bible and today You spoke to me about forgiveness. In the Bible it says, Be kind and compassionate to one another, forgiving each other, just as in Christ God forgave you. This is in Ephesians 4:32. I had to know that for today. Then I went to put on my Rocky clothes so I could do my moves. But I did not feel like doing my moves and instead I wanted to eat because I was hungry. I went to the refrigerator and I wanted to make eggs, but there were no eggs. Emily was sleeping, so I took money on the counter and I went to the store. God, it is easy because the store is only one block from home. Nobody was in the store except for me and some people. One of the other people was a mom. I did not know her, but I did know her. She is the mother of Alex Miller. Alex Miller killed people. He was the shooter. He died. His mother is Miss Miller. Nobody likes her.

I know this because I know it.

Also I know this because Emily told me.

And I know this because I saw it.

I saw Miss Miller and she saw me too. I have seen Miss Miller many times in life but I do not remember because I do not write it down. I do not know Miss Miller. I do not hate her. You said love everyone, God, so that is what I do. She did not make Alex kill people. But people blame her. They still blame her. That is what happened when I saw her today. I went to the egg part of the store because I wanted eggs. I was getting eggs and I saw Miss Miller. She was afraid, God. She stopped. She held her breath in. I did not want her to be scared so I did not do anything. Then she looked like she wanted to cry. So I waved to her. Then I spoke. I said hello to her. She did not speak. I do not think she could. Something was wrong with her. I think she had a lot of sadness. Then I said more, and I do not know why I said what I said, but I said it. This is what I said.

I said, Miss Miller, I am not mad at you and God forgives You.

Miss Miller was quiet, and she cried and this was not a loud crying, but a quiet crying. I know this because I saw it. I saw her eyes. She did not say anything and she even smiled a little. Then something bad happened. There was someone else there. It was a man who was mad. He called Miss Miller a name that nobody should ever call anyone ever in life. I cannot say it since it is bad.

I said to him, That is bad and also a false.

Then he called me a retard and he left.

I looked back to Miss Miller but she was gone. She left her cart and all her stuff. God, I prayed for her there. I pray she is okay and not sad. I pray Miss Miller knows she is forgiven. I pray that everyone knows they are forgiven.

All they have to do is ask.

Nineteen

A PRAYER FOR MY FRIENDS AND MY ENEMIES

God, my friends need you.

But so do my enemies.

I will pray for them all.

I am going to pray first for my enemies. I have a reason to pray for them. Today is a Red Day Friday. Today was a good day. But I was thinking about all the people I like. And I wanted to pray for them. But I also remember in the Bible it says to love your enemies. In the Bible it says, But I tell you, love your enemies and pray for those who persecute you. It is from Matthew 5:44. That is why I will pray for my enemies. I am going to pray now. First, I will pray for Morton the fat man who looks grossly at Izzy. I do not like him, God. He is a bad person. I pray You change his heart and that he gets a good heart. I pray he would stop looking at Izzy grossly and instead takes care of her. I pray that Morton also takes care of my friends, Ernie and Ira. If not then I pray You make justice on him. God, next I pray for Sandra who used to know Emily but is no longer her friend. Sandra was mean to me and it still hurts me and sometimes I think about it, but I forgive her. Sometimes I see Sandra when I am out and she stares at me and I know that she hates me a lot. Sometimes I remember what she did and it makes me want to hate her, but I will not. I hate what she did, but I do not hate her. The only thing I will hate is evil. I pray that Sandra is no longer mean and that she would be good. God, I pray next for Jacob. He sucks. I do not like him at all. But Jesus said to love everyone, so I will pray for him too.

I pray he says sorry to Emily and that he knows what he did was wrong and then is good. I pray Jacob finds You, God, and that he leaves Emily alone forever and ever. I also pray that Jacob finds the purpose for his life and then he helps many people and himself. And if he does not then I pray You make big justice on him. That is because he sucks. Now I am done praying for my enemies.

I will pray for my friends now.

God, I pray all my friends get what they need. Sometimes I do not know what they need, but You know. I pray for Izzy, Ernie and Ira, and that they are set free from their prison at Morning Home. I also pray that Izzy gets the money that her parents are trying to steal. It is hers. I pray that Ernie finds a mom. His mom is dead and he misses her. I pray for Ira that he has forgiveness in his heart because he is angry at people and the world. Ira is mad because the world is mean and has been mean to him, but he has also done bad things. I pray for Pastor Nate because he is sad even if he does not look like it. Pastor Nate is sad nobody listens to him because he says things that are honest. Pastor Nate is also sad because he lost his family so I pray for his happiness. He never says this. It is okay, because I know it, and if I know it, I can pray for it. I know some other things too. Doctor Hemming needs prayers, and I pray that he knows You. He is in a bad hurt now. He has been in a bad hurt for many years since I became dumb. If he knows You, he will be okay. I also pray for Emily, God. I pray that she does not have to take care of me anymore. It is hard. She loves me and I love her. I want her to take care of me, but I also do not want this. I want her to be happy. I pray that she does not have to do it anymore, even if it means I cannot be with my sister anymore. I pray all these things come true.

I want to pray for myself now.

Sometimes it feels wrong.

But I think it is right.

I pray for a big thing now, God. I pray to be healed. I am sick and I am dumb. And I know I am getting sicker. They do not tell me, but I know. I know it in my heart and soul. It is something I can feel. I pray that I am healed and get to live a long, long, long time. But also I would rather just go to Heaven and be with You now. Living forever in Heaven will be more fun than now. I do not know what Heaven will be like. I think there is a big castle and many colors. I think You will tell me stories when I get there. I do not know. I do not think anyone knows. The Bible says this. What no eye has seen, what no ear has heard, and what no human mind has conceived, the things God has prepared for those who love him. This is from I Corinthians 2:9. This means I cannot know what You prepared for me in Heaven because it is too big and cool. Sometimes I think about things like this. I think of a thing like time. God, You created time. It is Yours. And if You can create time, then You can create something else like that, but something different. Also, You want to give things like that to us, and to me. This is what I pray for. I pray these things. I pray it will happen soon. I hope it is okay to pray this for myself.

Pastor Nate says it is okay to pray for me.

But I will keep praying for other people.

I hope someone is praying for me too.

Twenty

THE MOVIES and THE MINI MOVIES

God, I went to the movies today.

But I did not get to stay for the movie.

I only got to stay for the beginning.

I like beginnings. I like the Mini Movies. These are previews. I think I have told you this before. I do not remember. But I like them. Mini Movies are like dreams. They begin and they end, and sometimes you are not ready for the beginning and sometimes you are not ready for the ending, and you do not know where one ends and the other begins and that is why Mini Movies are like dreams. Sometimes when I see Mini Movies, I forget what movie I am going to see and I am surprised. Mini Movies can also be better than movies because sometimes the ending of a movie is not good. I think I like Mini Movies the best because they are the beginnings and beginnings are always good. When a movie begins it can be many different things and it could grow into a good thing. Sometimes at home I watch Mini Movies over and over and sometimes I watch the beginnings of movies over and over. I almost never get past the beginning.

God, I forgot what I wanted to tell you.

I am starting to have a bad memory.

I have to begin again.

It was a White Day Saturday and Emily and me always go to the movies on White Days, except for just one time. But now it is two times because today I had to go by myself. She said I had to stay home, but I said, No.

She said, What do you mean no?

I said, No.

She said, No?

I said, Today is a White Day and on White Day Saturdays we always go to the movies, so no.

She said, No, what?

I said, No.

She said, You need to stay home.

So I thought about what she said and there was a silence, because she said I needed to stay home before and then she said it again and I had to figure out if those things were different, but they were the same thing, so I was done with the silence and I said, No. And then I said, Today is a White Day and on White Day Saturdays we always go to the movies, so no.

Emily sat on the couch and looked at the floor and rubbed the sides of her head with her fingers and did not talk, even though she wanted to talk more. She had madness. I know she had madness because she only does this when she is trying to figure out what to say because she has madness. She looked up and the sun was on her face from the window, and her face was all sparkly.

I said, Emily, your face is all sparkly.

She said, What are you talking about?

I said, Why is your face all sparkly?

I asked this because Emily only has a sparkly face when she goes out to meet other boys who she likes and sometimes does not like. Emily stood up and got her purse, and she pulled a bunch of money out of her purse. She told me to hold out my hand so I did. She placed a bunch of money in my hand.

She said, I can't go to the movies with you today, I'm sorry.

I wanted to cry, but I did not. I did not say anything because I was afraid I would cry and if I cry then Emily will cry or get madness so I did not.

She said, Don't be like that, Todd.

But still I did not say anything.

She said, It'll be fun for you, getting to go by yourself.

But still I did not say anything.

Then she said, You just need to take the bus, you can do that.

But still I did not say anything.

She said, It's easy, just take this money, this is fifty dollars, go to the movies, you can see whatever you want, and next weekend we'll go together.

I said, We always go to the movies on White Days except just one time.

She said, You're thirty-three, you can take the bus and go by yourself.

But I saw my reflection in the living room mirror, and I saw me, I was seven, and I wanted to say this but I knew she would get madness so I did not.

Emily rubbed my hair and said goodbye and left. And my face hurt and so did my chest. I remembered Doctor Hemming and Pastor Nate had told me to control my feelings so I did. But I was not happy because on White Days Emily and me always go to the movies except just one time, and now that is a false.

I stood still.

Then I thought for a long time.

I had many thoughts in my head.

It was loud in my head. I did not know what to do. It is different when I write it, God. When I write, all my thoughts are in a list and I see it. But when I was standing still it was all at once. God, it was too many thoughts all at once in my head. I had madness because I had to figure out too many things. I had to figure out what to wear. I had to figure out what sneakers to wear. I had to figure out what movie to see. I had to figure out what time to go. I had to make sure the lights in the house were off. I had to make sure the stove was off. I had to remember to lock all the doors. I had to remember to not forget the money. I had to figure out how to get to the movie theater at the mall. I had to figure out how to get back home from the movie theater at the mall and since the mall is far away that means home is also far away from the mall. I had to make sure the phone Emily gave me for emergencies only was charged. Also, God, the other voices were back, and they talked while I was thinking. The voices were making me afraid and they said things I want to forget. They said things I do not want to write, but I will, and they said that I was too dumb to go to the movies myself. They said I cannot even pick out a shirt to wear. They said I would mess up and leave the lights on and leave the stove on. They said I would burn the house down.

They said I would forget to lock the door and someone would rob our house and that the stove would blow up and the house would burn down and then we would not have a home and it would be my fault and I would get in trouble and Emily would have madness and leave me forever. So I got madness and yelled and threw the money. And then I got quiet. But I still did not know what to do.

So I prayed.

I prayed for You to help me, because I knew You would. You are always helping me and taking care of me. But the other voices I did not like kept coming back and they said bad things I definitely will not write. So then I prayed out loud and louder than the voices could talk. I said, God, I am sorry for yelling and throwing the money but I need help because I do not know what to do next. I still had madness because I could not do anything by myself. Then You reminded me I did not have to do it by myself. Because I am not God, I am just Todd. So I stayed there and did not do anything for a long time.

I prayed one more time.

And I waited and waited. I did this because the Bible says so. It says, Be still before the Lord, and wait patiently for Him. This is in Psalm 37:7. God I knew You would do something because You love me and know me. So I waited.

Then I waited some more.

You did not change anything.

But You showed me something.

God, You showed me a Mini Movie of me. I saw me waiting at the bus stop. I had the money in my pocket and I was wearing my button shirt and a sweater over that shirt because it was cold outside. I was holding the phone that Emily has given me for emergencies only. I was wearing my best, nice, white sneakers. I had a list in my other hand and the list told me to do these things. The list also said to take the bus to the movies and turn off the lights, to check that the stove was off and lock the door. I saw everything on the list crossed off and that means that I did it. Then I remembered in the Bible it says, Call to me and I will answer you and tell you great and unsearchable things you do not know. This is from Jeremiah 33:3. This was a great and unsearchable thing so I said thank You, God, because You always help. I was happy and had no more madness.

So I did exactly what You said.

I made a list and wrote out all the things to do.

Then I did them.

It was easy because I remembered what You showed me. I picked the money off the floor and put it in my pocket. I put on my button shirt and my sweater over that because it is cold outside. I held the phone that Emily gave me for emergencies. I put on my best, nice, white sneakers. I turned off the lights, and then I made sure the stove was off, and then I locked the door and I walked outside. I walked to the end of the block where the bus stop is and did not get lost. This is where I waited for the bus. I looked at the list I made and everything was crossed off. It looked like the Mini Movie in my head.

I did not know what came after.

This made me afraid.

But I was brave.

The bus stopped so I got on it. Nobody else was on it. It was just me and the bus driver. He had a Bible next to his seat, so I know that the bus driver was from You. It was good. I have seen him at church. I do not know his name. He is an older man. I do not know how old he is and Emily says it is not nice to ask things like that to people so I did not.

I said, Hello, my name is Todd, I am seven, but I am also thirty-three.

The man laughed and said, Okay, hello, Todd.

I said, I have seen you at my church, but I do not know your name.

He laughed again and said, My name is Roger.

I said, Hello, Roger. I am going to see a movie. Today is a White Day.

He said, I have no idea what that means but I can bring you to the movie theater at the mall. Is that where you need to go?

I told him okay and said thank you. I stood and neither of us said anything for a little bit and it was weird. He looked at the empty seat and then I did too and then I looked back at him.

He said, Would you like to sit down, Todd?

I told him yes, and then I sat down.

And Roger drove the bus to the mall.

On the way to the mall I was thinking.

I like to do this and listen to my mixtapes.

So I thought and listened to my White Day mixtape.

Sometimes I think wrong things. Sometimes when I think something, it is not what I wanted to think, so I ask for forgiveness. I do this because I have thought something wrong about You, God, and You are my father and I love You like I love my father. I love You because You saved me from hell and because You died for my sins. I love You because You brought me back to life when I died, and You will do it again when I die. I love You because You forgive me when I ask for forgiveness. I also love You because You said, Be strong and courageous. Do not be afraid or terrified because of them, for the Lord your God goes with you; he will never leave you nor forsake you. This is in Deuteronomy 31:6. You promised. You do not lie. This is why I love You and You know my thoughts so I will think good.

If you love someone, you do not want to do things that make them feel bad, you tell them you are sorry when you did something wrong. And you want to talk to them all the time. If you love someone then you want to do many things that will make them happy. God, I forgot I was writing to You. Now I remember, this is why I love You. It is why I ask for forgiveness for bad thoughts.

You also help me think.

Thinking is hard. Thinking can be dangerous too. Sometimes I do not want to think because there are sad things I have to think about. But You always help me when I have to think them. That is what I did when I thought and listened to my White Day mixtape. I did not have many thoughts until I heard one song I really, really like. On my White Day mixtape there is a song by a person named Prince and the song is about rain. This is the song I was listening to. Emily says this is her favorite favorite song in the entire whole world. I like this song too, but not as much as Emily likes it. And I was listening to this song and thought about Emily and why she did not go to the movies with me today. We always go to the movies on White Days except just one time. I know this because I checked The Calendar of Todd. This time was Saturday, May Eighteenth, Two Thousand and Two. That day I was in the living room on the floor watching television and waiting to go to the movies with Emily. That day she walked to me and was crying.

That day I said, Emily, why are you crying?

She said, Todd, we can't go to the movies today.

I said, But Emily, we always go to the movies on White Days.

She said, Today we can't.

I said, Why?

She said, Because mom went to Heaven today.

Emily hugged me and we cried. But we were also happy because we know mom is in Heaven. We know mom is in Heaven because she asked Jesus Christ to be the Master of her life. She did this the same day I did. I remember this time because I just do. I remember we went to church that day because my mom said we needed to go, and we had never been even once in my entire whole life. She said she did not know why we had to go, but that we just had to go. So we went. God, after I asked Jesus Christ to forgive me of my sins and be Master of my life, my mom did too, and then Emily did too. We will all be together in Heaven with You one day, and my dad too because he already did this. I know this because You do not lie, and the Bible says that if You say with your mouth that Jesus is Lord and believe in your heart that God raised him from the dead then you will be saved. This is from Romans 10:9. That is why I know we will be with You forever. That is why Emily and me did not go to the movies that time. This made me cry. Sometimes I think a sad thing because sometimes I have to. Sometimes I cry. Sometimes I fall asleep crying. That is what I did.

Then I woke up. Waking up is like starting over. Sometimes I wake up in the morning and things do not go good, and then later I sleep and wake up and I get to do it over. This morning I woke up and things did not go good, but it got better, and now I am doing it over. But I think I was crying in my sleep because my eyes were wet. Roger had his hand on my shoulder.

He said, Todd, you okay?

I was not okay. I was afraid, but I did not say anything. I was afraid because Roger was supposed to be driving, but he had his hand on my shoulder, so I did not know who was driving the bus. I looked out the window though and I saw the mall. Also, the bus was not moving, so then I was not afraid. Roger told me this was my stop and he asked if I was okay again. So I told him I was okay.

But I lied.

Because I was still not okay. I lied because it is weird to tell a person you just met why you are crying. So I wiped my eyes and my nose. I told Roger it was nice to meet him, because it was nice to meet him. I got off the bus. Maybe one day Roger and I will be friends. I think he cares. Some people do not. This made me want to sleep more. Sometimes when you wake up, it is sad because you wish you were still dreaming, and you know you have to start over.

Now I was at the mall.

I did not know what to do next because I was afraid again. I was afraid because the mall is big. I was not lost because the mall was right in front of me. But I was afraid because inside the mall I might get lost and I have no photos of inside the mall. And then I would not know how to get home and that makes me afraid. There are also lots of people at the mall. Some of them are from Morning and some of them are from other towns I do not know. Some of them are not nice. Emily has been bringing me here since when I was smart. One time we saw a man fight another man and throw a burger at his face and then they punched each other. It was a bad fight. Another time some kids called me a bad word that I will not say. Emily was in the bathroom and I never told her. Another time a woman in sunglasses bumped into me and dropped her bags and she yelled at me and called me a retard. Emily was in the dressing room when it happened. I did not tell her that because another time, this man called me a retard while Emily was getting popcorn for us, and she came back with popcorn and asked why I looked sad, and I said that person called me a retard, so she went over to him and pushed him and then she threw a soda in his face and she threw popcorn at him and also she punched him in the head but nobody saw that. He was dumb and swore and then he tried to punch Emily and people saw that so he got kicked out of the movies. We did not get kicked out because nobody saw Emily punch him and she told me not to tell anyone so I never did. We got more popcorn, but Emily had madness the rest of the day. The mall is a place you should not go alone. It is full of kids who swear, women who have madness, and men who are dumb. The mall is a dangerous place, full of evil and bad people who sometimes call you retard or other bad words. But sometimes it is also fun.

I went inside this place. But I got afraid and turned around. Then I went inside again. When I got inside the mall I did not know where I had to go. There were lots of people. I was where all the food places are. Some people stared at me. One girl bumped into me and called me a name I will not say because it is a bad word. She had black hair. She was skinny. She was much younger than Emily. She was pretty, but she was evil, so I did not like her at all. I remember in King Arthur there is an evil woman with black hair, and this person was like her. Sometimes people can be pretty on the outside but evil on the inside. She pushed me away and I tripped over my feet, but I did not fall. I walked away fast but I did not know where to go. God, I remembered that we are supposed to pray for our enemies, and I did not want to do this. But You said to do it so I prayed for the Evil Girl. I said, God, I do not want to pray for the Evil Girl because she sucks, but You said to, so I will, so please make the Evil Girl not evil, because she is mean to me and she is evil, and maybe now she will be good. I felt good. I looked up and I saw the movie theater was right ahead. So that is where I went. I think the Evil Girl was meant to get me where I was supposed to be. That reminded me that You always know where I need to go. Even if a bad thing happens, You know how to turn it into a good thing.

That is how I got to the movie theater.

But I forgot that Emily was not with me. I was alone. I remembered that I was alone, and I had madness, but then I controlled all my feelings. I wanted to cry, but I only did a little. I did a good job, and wiped my eyes, and I stopped crying. The Ticket Person asked if I wanted a ticket and I said yes. The Ticket Person was nice. He had a nose ring and long hair. He asked me what movie I wanted to see, but I did not know. I told him that Emily always tells me the movies because I do not read good. He asked me who Emily was.

I said, Emily is my sister.

He said, Is that her?

Then he pointed behind me. I turned and was happy because I thought Emily was behind me. But she was not.

It was the Evil Girl.

I said, No, that is the Evil Girl.

The Evil Girl heard me call her the Evil Girl. She got madness. This time she called me a freak, which is not a swear word, but it is mean. Then the Ticket Person called her a swear word back and then she called him a swear word too. The Ticket Person said to forget the Evil Girl, but she kept swearing. I pretended she was not there, but this was hard, because she was behind me being mean. The Ticket Person said not to look at her so I looked only at the Ticket Person. He read all the movies to me like Emily does. I picked one. I think it was a Star Wars movie. I do not remember. The Ticket Person asked me where I wanted to sit and I told him I wanted to sit in the middle. He said I could. So I gave the Ticket Person money, and he gave me money back and I got a ticket for the movie. I was happy now so it was easy to control my feelings.

I went farther inside.

I was at the middle part.

This is where they give you popcorn.

I like popcorn, but I did not deserve it because I was a coward. God, a coward is a person who runs when he should not. The Evil Girl was mean and said things that made me angry. If I was not a coward, I would have done something to her. But I was a coward. So I asked for forgiveness in my head because there were people around, and I said, God, I am sorry for being a coward and I ask You for forgiveness. I know You forgave me, because Pastor Nate says once you ask for forgiveness and you are serious, then it is over.

I got to the popcorn counter. I like this part. I like snacks. The Popcorn Girl was a good person. I know because I do.

The Popcorn Girl said, I know you, we go to the same church.

I said I was sorry because I did not know her.

She said, It's okay, I'm Lucy.

I said, My name is Todd, I am thirty-three but also seven.

She said, I know who you are, Todd. I am seventeen, but also seventeen.

Then she laughed.

I said, I do not understand.

She said it was a joke, but I did not understand because it was not funny. Then she asked what I wanted and I asked for a big popcorn and a big soda.

She told me I could have it. Then she laughed and so did I. I do not know why, but this was funny. I gave Lucy money and she gave me money back. She gave me a big popcorn and a big soda. But the Evil Girl came back and swore again, and Lucy swore at the Evil Girl. Lucy told the Evil Girl to stop it or Lucy would get her boss. I wanted to say something, but I did not because I did not know what to say. Lucy and the Evil Girl kept yelling and I did not know what to do, God, so I left. I was sad because I was still a coward.

I went farther inside.

It got darker. And darker. It got even darker, and I was afraid You left me. But You said that You never would, so I knew You were still there. The Ticket Ripper took my tickets and he ripped them. The Ticket Ripper was a big guy with a beard. He was tall. He told me to go to the first theater, but there was a theater on one side and a theater on the other. I told him I did not understand because there was two theaters and I did not know which came first. He told me to follow him, so I followed him inside the theater, and we went up the stairs to the middle seat. He pointed at a seat and told me it was mine and said to enjoy the movie. He left. And I said, Thank You, God, for bringing me here. That is when I knew You did not leave me because You did not leave me.

The lights turned dark.

I forgot I was a coward. I remembered that I was at the movies and I was happy. The screen made a pop noise, and the Mini Movies played. It was like being in a dream. When I am in a dream, I do not know it. And sometimes I go from one dream to the next, to the next, to the next, and it is fun. And I also forgot what movie I was going to see and that is the best, God. It is good because then the movie is a surprise movie. I was waiting to see what movie it was going to be and I was happy. And then something hit me. It hit my head and it hurt. I did not understand. And I got hit again and then it hurt again. I did not know where it was coming from. I did not know if it was real. Sometimes I cannot tell if I am making things up in my head. It made me afraid because I did not know what happened. I got hit again in the back of my head again so I stood up and turned around and I got hit in the face with candy. I know because I picked it up off the ground. And then I got hit in the face again and there were some people laughing and I could not see because I got hit in the eyes and it hurt. So I rubbed my eyes and I heard laughing and I saw who it was, God. It was the Evil Girl and she was laughing with someone in the back and they were throwing things at me, and I got hit in the face again and dropped my popcorn and I tried to catch it but I could not catch it and it went everywhere and then when I tried to catch it I hit my soda because my soda was in the cup holder and it got knocked out and I spilled my soda and the soda went all over the floor and also on me too, and I tripped and fell and I got up and ran away and I ran away fast.

I ran out of the theater.

Then I ran through the mall.

And I ran outside to the bus stop.

I had madness. I also remembered I was a coward. And the bus was there so I got on. And Roger was there. He asked why I was crying. I said I was okay. But God, I was not okay. I had so much madness. The voices came back and they said I should have madness at You, and they said terrible things and I thought I was mad at You. I had much madness, but no madness at You. You are the only one who knows me. I asked for forgiveness in my head over and over again because of my thoughts. And then Roger started driving and asked me if I wanted to talk, but I could not. I had too much madness. I was crying but I did not want to. Madness makes people do things they do not want to do. If there is madness, there is also sadness. That is because madness is sadness but different. I did not want to have sadness and madness because they are bad.

But sadness is not for always.

And madness is not for always.

Because this life is not for always.

The next life is for always. This makes me happy. It is the end, but it is not the end. There is much more. And it seems far away, but it is not. Sometimes I can almost see what it will be like. It is like the sun rising fast and all at once. It is like stars at night when I can see lots of them. Sometimes I see it when Emily hugs me, or when Izzy smiles, or when Ernie slaps my hand, or when Ira ruffles my hair. Sometimes I see it when I look in the mirror and I see the smart me I am supposed to be. And I always see it when You are talking to me.

Sometimes I also see it when I dream with my eyes open and think about things that are not real in this life, but maybe in the next. So I did this on the bus. I listened to my White Day mixtape. I listened to the song by Prince about rain again and I dreamed. I dreamed I was the president and helped all people. I dreamed I was a pilot and could fly high above the clouds, closer to You, God. I dreamed I was a doctor and saved people from dying. I dreamed I was a knight and fought against goblins. But none of these are a truth. They are only dreams.

They are previews in my mind.

Things not in this life.

But maybe in the next.

Twenty-One

LIGHT IN THE DARKNESS

I do not always understand You.

Because You are ununderstandable.

But sometimes I do understand You.

There are many things I do not understand. And sometimes the Bible says many things I do not understand. But then sometimes I think about it and then I do understand and that is because You let me understand. I do not know many things, but one thing I do know is that You are for Forever, and that is why you are ununderstandable. That means You do not end.

I also know another thing.

I know who You are.

The Bible tells me.

It says in the Bible that God is love, and I did not always understand this. And then I did understand this. But before I understood this, I thought about it and thought You were the thing that Emily has for Doctor Hemming, and I did not understand this. This made no truth. So I asked Pastor Nate and he told me what Emily has for Doctor Hemming is love but it is a romantic love. This makes me feel weird. You are not that kind of love. Pastor Nate said You are the Highest Kind of Love. It is sacrifice love. This is a different thing. It means You are like a father and You defend people and it is the best kind of love. There are other loves but I do not understand them. Now I understand what You are.

Now I know what love is.

Love is how I go see Izzy even though I am afraid. Love is how Emily takes care of me even though she does not want to. Love is how Doctor Hemming and Pastor Nate keep seeing me for many years even though I get worser. Love is how when I pray and keep praying and do not give up even though I hear bad things when I pray sometimes and even though sometimes I am angry. Love is how You talk to me and take care of me even though I have bad thoughts. Love is how You protect people You care about no matter what even if they do not understand. That is what You did when You became Jesus Christ when You died on the cross and protected us from going to hell. That is how people can go to Heaven. Now I understand love. Love is how You make a way.

You are always making a way.

Sometimes the way is blocked.

But You always find new ways.

The way to my home was blocked when Roger took me home. Roger took many streets, but they were all blocked. There was lots of rain and all the streets were blocked with cops and they said it might flood. Many streetlights were out and there was no light except from cop cars and the bus. Roger wanted to get me home because it was rainy, but I said I could make it from the bus stop. He said it was nonsense. I said no, it is sense. He said no and that he wanted to bring me all the way to Home Home. I told him, Thanks, but you cannot do that because Emily is not home yet. Roger did not understand. So I said that Home Home means when Emily is home. Then Roger understood. And then I said that but even when it is Home Home, it is not Truth Home, it is just Now Home because Now Home is a place you live right now, but it is not Truth Home.

He said, What is Truth Home?

I told him that Truth Home means Heaven. Roger nodded. And then I told him that nobody can get to Truth Home themselves, only Jesus Christ can take them. He said that he knew that, but he enjoyed the reminder.

He said, Todd, you know what, you're a good one.

I said, A good what?

He said, A good one.

I said, Thank you. You are a good one also.

Then he said, Look at that.

I said, Look at what?

He said, It stopped raining.

Then he drove to a street and a cop let him go through. He dropped me off at my Now Home and said goodbye. I said goodbye back. I went inside my house. It was home, but it was only Now Home.

This was not Home Home.

It was just a dark house with nobody inside. I turned on the lights. I saw me in the living room mirror. I saw myself which is a seven-year-old. But my eyes could not see right because I was rubbing them. I only saw blurry things. I had a thought when I saw with blurry eyes. My thought was this, God. My thought was that this world is like a mirror. I also read in the Bible once where it says, For now we see through a glass, darkly; but then face to face: now I know in part; but then shall I know even as also I am known. This is from I Corinthians 13:12. I know what this means because You told me. You said that it means that this world is not a Truth World. I understand this. I do not understand many things, but You had me understand. You always do, God. Because in life it is like I am always walking around in the dark, but then You turn the lights.

But Your Light is different.

Your Light is a Good Light. Your Light is a Truth Light. I have seen this light only two times in my entire whole life. One time was when I was at the old movie theater that one night where they do not play movies anymore, and there was darkness but I saw Your Light. I also saw Your Light the day I died and everything was dark but then it was bright. I know it was Your Light because I just do. I want to see Your Light again.

That is when I saw it again.

I saw it outside my home.

It was shining.

Your Light was outside. I saw it through the window. So I went outside. But I got outside and it was gone. I did not know where it was and I looked all over and spun in a circle. I could not find it. And then I found it. I saw Your Light. It looked like a person who was bright light at the end of the street and glowing.

I did not know who this was, but I know this person was good. I know because I just do. I know the same way I know You are God. That is because You told me. One time, a long time ago, Pastor Nate told me about the Holy Trinity, but I did not understand. So I went home and I said, God, I do not understand the Holy Trinity, will You tell me? And You did and You told me in the way where I just know. And I knew that You are God who is All Things, and I knew that Jesus Christ is also You and that You made Yourself as a human so we would all know You and love You, and I knew that because You are God You have a Spirit which is You.

So when I saw the person at the end of the street I knew this person was good because I just did. And I knew to follow the glowing person. So I did. The glowing person walked and I did too, but the glowing person was ahead of me. I followed the glowing person many blocks all the way to the old movie theater under the streetlight. Then the glowing person was gone.

It got dark.

Like a storm.

It was a darkness storm.

God, You are always surprising me. You are always making things happen different even though sometimes the same thing is happening. It is like You are giving me a test You want me to pass. Because the mean wind came back.

But I do not think this was You, God.

This time the mean wind was all darkness. It was like the night, but not the night, it was worser. And the mean wind was not wind, it was worser and windyer. This darkness was a dumb darkness, like when people have too much beer. It moved like it was too heavy. And this darkness made bad things and said bad things. I could see things in the dark. I will not say what I saw but it was scary. This darkness touched the streetlight and the pole rusted. The streetlight got hit by the darkness and it cracked and broke and the glass fell to the ground. But the glass did not hurt me. The glass fell on both sides of me because that is how it fell. God, I think that is because You protected me. You did this because You are good to me. But it got even darker. It was darker than it has ever been in my entire whole life. I could see some things. They said bad things I should not say. They said You hated me. They said You made me dumb. They said I should have madness and that I should take that madness and be mad at You. I am sorry, but I had madness at You. It was a short madness. But it was still madness and I asked for forgiveness. They said more bad things. They said You had a bad plan for my life and I should be afraid of all the bad things in my future. But in the Bible it is different than that. The Bible says, "For I know the plans I have for you," declares the Lord, "plans to prosper you and not to harm you, plans to give you a hope and a future." This is from Jeremiah 29:11. And God does not lie ever. So I knew the darkness was a liar. But it was all darkness. I could not see anything in front of my face. So I said, God please help me. And You did.

The Light above me turned on.

It was the streetlight.

It glowed.

It did not have a light because it blew up, but it glowed anyway. The light was the brightest bright light I have ever seen in my entire whole life. That is because it was a Truth Light which is light from Heaven. Truth Light is Your Light. The Truth Light shined all over me. It was a force field. It was a Truth Light Force Field. God, a force field is a laser shield so bad guys cannot get inside and they die when they touch it. It is like in X-Men when Jean Grey uses her mind to make a force field energy ball. The Truth Light Force Field was warm inside. The bad voices were still there though. Also, it was dark outside the Truth Light Force Field, and I could not see anywhere. But Your Truth Light made a sidewalk to the movie theater door and I followed it. The bad voices were screaming and yelling the worst things I have heard in my entire whole life. They tried to break into the Truth Light Force Field, but they could not do it. I saw darkness hit the Truth Light Force Field and I saw the darkness burn away like smoke. Then I heard the darkness scream because the Truth Light Force Field hurt it. When the darkness figured out it could not hurt me in the Truth Light Force Field, they said more lies. The voices said I would be safe in darkness and that You would burn me. God, I am dumb, but I am not stupid. The darkness is a bunch of liars who made me have madness. They were telling me to be afraid. But, I was not. I followed the Light sidewalk to the movie theater door. The door opened to more Truth Light and it was so bright I could not see and the door shut behind me.

I felt like I was Truth Home.

But I was not Truth Home.

I was at a movie theater.

I was at the movies with many other people. I felt really good and happy. I was at the middle part of the movies when people get popcorn and soda and candy and stuff. I saw myself in the mirror where the candy is. I looked like I always do, like a seven-year-old. Then I heard all these people talking. Some were in line and some were eating popcorn and candy. Some were in circles with their friends laughing, but they were all friends. They were having a happy time because they were at the movies. The people looked at me. They looked at me for a long time and they were all quiet. It was quieter than ever before in my entire whole life. Human people could never be that quiet. But these people were not human people. Because that is when I noticed what they really were.

They were Angels.

They all had armor on. They were all bright. They did not have wings but they did have swords and shields. The Angel that was closest to me had long brown hair and muscles that were as big as me. He had gold armor pants on too. God, this Angel had a sword that had bright blue energy around it like in Star Wars, but it was a real sword and not a laser. God, this Angel had words on his armor, but I could not read it. Angels are cool. Angels speak a different language. This is the language of Heaven.

I know because one Angel talked to me.

This Angel said many things to me. But I was afraid. I did not know if I could trust him. The Bible says the devil dresses up as an angel of light. So that is why I was afraid. This Angel told me that his words were being translated by God to me so I could understand him. This Angel said I was welcome here in this place. This Angel said I was my true self here. This Angel said he knew I was going to introduce myself and say I was thirty-three but also seven, except that my true self is only seven-years-old. This Angel said more things, but that is when I covered my ears and said, I do not want to hear. The Angel asked me why, and I said because in the Bible it says the devil dresses up as an angel of light so I do not know if I can trust you and maybe you are the devil and I just do not know.

Then the Angel smiled. He looked at the other Angels. All the Angels smiled, and then the Angels laughed. These were good laughs, not evil laughs. The Angel said I did not have to worry about the devil here. When the Angel said this, his breath blew my Blue Day hat off and I almost fell because I am small and Angels are tall. The Angels laughed and the one I was talking to picked me up. He said his name was Raphael. He lifted me by my shirt and put me on the countertop where they get popcorn and candy and soda and stuff, and he put my hat back on me.

Then I heard a trumpet.

It was so loud I had to cover my ears. All the Angels kneeled. They were all quiet. And the room disappeared. And the roof went away and turned into space, but it was not space, it was clouds and mountains and sky and stars like I had never seen. It was pretty and the ground turned into white stone and shining glass. All the Angels were still kneeling.

There was Light.

It was Truth Light. But even way more bright than the Truth Light I had seen before. I had only seen this light once in my life, and that is when I died and went to the Secret Place. This was the same light. In the Light was a Person. It was You and You were Jesus Christ. You were brighter than the Angels. I could not see because You were so bright. I know it was You because I just do. But I got afraid. I looked down because I did not want to do something wrong and give You madness. I thought of all the bad things that had ever been in my head and I thought You were going to be mad. So I looked down. You laughed. This was not a bad laugh, it was a good laugh, and You laughed loud. The laugh was so loud I had to cover my ears again, but for some reason my ears did not hurt. You waved to the Angels. You spoke to them in a language I did not know, but I knew. You told them to rise. They stood up all at once and made a bang when they stood because their feet were loud, and they made another bang when they tapped their shields three times on the ground, and they did this at the same time. Then I saw how many Angels stood behind You, and there was more Angels than a person could ever count in a hundred entire whole lifes. They were a great army. You spoke to them, but You did not open Your Mouth. You said to them that I thought You were mad at me. The Angels laughed, and You did too. The laughing was so loud that the ground was shaking, but it did not hurt my ears. The Angels stopped laughing and You were smiling. Then You spoke to me. You spoke, but I heard no words. You did not open Your Mouth. You spoke in my heart. I heard You in my mind. I heard it inside every part of my entire whole self. You said You were not mad at me. You said You forgave me a long time ago, and nothing will ever change that, not even the powers of hell. Then I saw Your Eyes. There was fire in Your Eyes. You said were proud of me for being brave. You said You were proud of me for always doing my best. You said I was handpicked from before the creation of the entire whole world. And You said I was faithful. You said You had an important mission, and it was just for me. I was still looking at the floor. You told me to lift my head and stand up so I did that.

You Spoke out loud this time.

It was a different language.

I did not know it, but I knew it.

You Spoke to me and it was ununderstandable but I understood. You told me You had been helping me write my book because I could not do it by myself, especially the ending. You said You would keep helping me write it, but I would not know it, and I would soon forget You were helping me so I said thank You.

Then I saw how tall You were.

You were way taller than any human person and way bigger than the entire whole universe. I could not see it, but I knew it. You also had scars on Your Hands and You said the scars were for me. You held my hand. I cried. I cried because You made me understand You loved me bigger than the entire whole world, and the entire whole universe, and You loved me before I was born also. You said You love me now and forever. You told me this in Your Language.

It was ununderstandable, but I understood it.

Then You showed me more things. I do not remember it but I remember. First You showed me things about me and I saw my whole life from beginning to ending but then You made me forget it. You said I would remember when it was time to remember and I said okay. It was like a Mini Movie. Then You showed me something new. You made a window from nothing and You opened the window, and inside the window was a new place. You told me it was Heaven. You told me

I could look. So I did and I saw Heaven. I cannot say what it looked like because You made me forget and You said it was for my own good. But I remember You said this was a new story. I remember this story did not have a beginning, and You said this story will never end. Then I cried for a long, long time. I cried for hundreds and hundreds of years, but I never ever got old. I cried even longer than that and You never left me, You were always there. Because even though I did not understand, I still did understand. This is why I cried. Sometimes crying is not a bad thing. Sometimes crying can be a happy thing. I think good stories are like that. Sometimes, stories make you cry, and sometimes they make you happy. Sometimes stories make you cry and you are happy at the same time, and it is a good feeling, and you do not know why but you still do know why, and they are ununderstandable stories and you do not want them to end ever.

I understand now.

This is sort of what You are like. You are like an ununderstandable story, without any beginning or end that is for always, and when I think about this I cry and I am happy at the same time and I do not know why, but I still do know why.

This is a good feeling.

PRESENTING A MINI MOVIE EPISODE OF
THE ADVENTURES OF TODD

IN

TODD
and
THE QUEST FOR THE HOLY GRAIL

A Medieval EPIC
Part I
A Mini Movie by Todd

written for the screen by
Todd Carpenter on
Monday
September 8th,
1997

OVER BLACK.

The projector spins up and the film rolls. A pop marks the
synthesis of celluloid and sound, and with it comes the
disembodied, ambiguously deep --

British Trailer voice.

                    NARRATOR (V.O.)
               In the year of our Lord,
               Five hundred and Twenty-Two,
               on the island of Great Britain,
               in the Kingdom of Camelot,
               there ruled the greatest regent of
               all England --

KING ARTHUR.

Close on his face, the edge of the sword named Excalibur held
tight between the eyes of this fifty-year-old ruler.

                    NARRATOR (V.O.)
               King Arthur.

He stands on a raised platform in the idyllic courtyard.
By his side stands MERLIN the elderly wizard.
The king levels Excalibur outward toward --

KNIGHTS OF THE ROUNDTABLE.

All two hundred of them in formation, standing before the
King. They bow in unison, and move into a kneeling position
with their heads low.

                    NARRATOR (V.O.)
               The ruler who ordered upon his
               knights the greatest quest of all
               time.

                    KING ARTHUR
               I now commence the greatest quest
               of all time: the quest for the Holy
               Grail. Who will be my champion?
               What say you?

Whispers and murmurs among them, and none move.

                    NARRATOR (V.O.)
               But when none show the courage to
               step forth, one hero emerges.

FLASH --

A blinding flare of **LIGHTNING** from the clear blue sky *strikes* between King Arthur and the kneeling knights --
the ground **EXPLODES** with dirt and dust --

KING ARTHUR.

Waving away the smoke from his face as he attempts to get a good look at the damage to reveal --

A BRIGHT SPHERE.

An energy cocoon-like pod, spherical with someone inside glowing, radiating, pulsating bright. The cocoon increases its intensity and brightness and --

ZAP --

It disappears at once leaving a young person with coiling electricity zap-zap zapping along his face and chest.

                NARRATOR (V.O.)
    His name --

TODD.

Age seven. Wearing his signature shirt, jeans and a baseball cap. The Knights stare in awe at this strange and supernatural event. Todd waves at them.

                NARRATOR (V.O.)
    Todd.

Todd waves to Arthur and Merlin --

                NARRATOR (V.O.)
    A boy sent from the future by God
    Himself.

                MERLIN
    This boy has been sent from the
    future by God Himself.

                NARRATOR (V.O.)
    To be the finder of the Holy Grail.

                MERLIN
    To be the finder of the Holy Grail.
    His eyes tell the story of courage.

Moving in tight on Todd's face, close to the eyes --

Now moving outward from his face -- the background behind
Todd has changed, so has his attire as he is now --

TODD THE KNIGHT.

Seven-year-old Todd now in full medieval shining armor.
He kneels in the courtyard and bows his head.
Excalibur taps his shoulder, knighted by --

KING ARTHUR.

> KING ARTHUR
> I knight thee: Sir Todd,
> Knight of the Morning.
> Rise.

Todd stands.

> NARRATOR (V.O.)
> Now he must journey forth into the
> Dark Lands. But not alone.

> KING ARTHUR
> Now you must journey forth into the
> Dark Lands. But not alone.

One knight steps at Todd's left side --

SIR IRONSIDE.

A warrior of massive proportions in his thirties. He looks a
lot like Ira. The sword on his back must weigh two hundred
pounds and he could swing it with ease. He has a handlebar
mustache and a buzzcut. He stands five feet taller than Todd.

> NARRATOR (V.O.)
> The iron knight, Sir Ironside,
> has been deemed first protector of
> Todd.

They nod to each other.

> KING ARTHUR
> The iron knight, Sir Ironside,
> I have deemed first protector of
> Todd.

At Todd's right side steps a second knight --

SIR ERNEST.

He has a young face in need of a shave, also in his thirties, with shoulder length blond hair and a normal, muscular frame. He looks identical to Ernie.

NARRATOR (V.O.)
The earnest knight, Sir Ernest, has been deemed second protector of Todd.

They nod to each other.

KING ARTHUR
The earnest knight, Sir Ernest, I have deemed second protector of Todd. But another is needed.

KING ARTHUR.

Holding Excalibur, the mythic sword, by the blade and the hilt, presenting the weapon of great power to --

TODD.

The boy accepts in a gracious and deferent bow. As he does, a rousing classical battle song plays in the background.

Todd turns to the knights.

He raises Excalibur.

The knights raise their swords in unison as later --

A HILLTOP.

The three knights on their horses viewed from far away trot along the crest of the knoll. The sun sets in the background.

NARRATOR (V.O.)
He ventures into the Dark Lands with Sir Ironside and Sir Ernest. and his superior horse --

TODD.

Feeding his horse some grass while Sir Ironside and Sir Ernest sit down by a fire.

                    TODD
          You will need a name.
          I shall call you --

A crack of thunder in the sky -- it catches Todd's attention.

                    NARRATOR (V.O.)
          Thunder Son.

                    TODD
          Thunder Son.

                    NARRATOR (V.O.)
          Now with his superior horse,
          Thunder Son, and his new friends,
          he must face ugly enemies of all
          kinds --

A GOBLIN.

In a dark forest, with sunken eyes and dark green weathered skin wielding a spiked club, runs toward Todd while Sir Ironside and Sir Ernest stand in front of Todd --

But Todd moves in front of them --

He unleashes Excalibur and SWINGS --

                    NARRATOR (V.O.)
          And defeat them --

THE DESERT.

Todd, Sir Ironside and Sir Ernest, all ride their horses slouched and parched, dying of thirst --

                    NARRATOR (V.O.)
          And travel to distant lands --

A CAVE.

Todd stands at the mouth of the cave, darkness before him, light behind him. He holds Excalibur in one hand, his horse's bridle rein strap in the other.

                    NARRATOR (V.O.)
          This is the quest for --
          THE HOLY GRAIL.

TODD.

Deep in the woods at night, now alone, holding the **Cup of Christ**, glowing in his hands, lighting up the entire forest.

>NARRATOR (V.O.)
>A tale of courage --

The soundtrack reaches a crescendo as --

TODD.

Riding on his horse fast along the British countryside with Sir Ernest and Sir Ironside beside him --
a cadre of **goblins** behind them --

>NARRATOR (V.O.)
>A tale of adventure --

TODD.

Standing side-by-side with Sir Ironside and Sir Ernest, surrounded by evil **goblins** --

>NARRATOR (V.O.)
>A tale of war.

Todd raises Excalibur and lunges toward the creatures --

>CUT TO BLACK.

>NARRATOR (V.O.)
>Todd and the Quest for the Holy Grail. Coming to a theater near you this summer. Rated PG thirteen.

TODD AND THE QUEST FOR THE HOLY GRAIL

FOREVERLAND ENTERTAINMENT PRESENTS
A FOREVERLAND ENTERTAINMENT PRODUCTION "TODD AND THE QUEST FOR THE HOLY GRAIL" A TODD CARPENTER MINI MOVIE
STARRING TODD CARPENTER KING ARTHUR SIR IRONSIDE THUNDER SON EXCALIBUR GOBLINS
DESIGN BY TODD
DISTRIBUTED BY FOREVERLAND ENTERTAINMENT

Twenty-Two
DREAMS AND REVELATIONS

I am happy.

I had a good dream.

But it was not a dream.

I had an adventure, but no one believed me. I told the person who found me sleeping in the road next to the theater. His name was Daniel. He did not believe me. He called the ambulance people, so I told them about my adventure, but they did not believe me either. When I got to the hospital, I told the nurses, but they also did not believe me. I told the doctor at the hospital who said his name was Doctor Coleman, but he did not believe me. Doctor Coleman said it sounded like quite an adventure, so I did not say anymore because I knew he did not believe me. I told them how I met Jesus Christ, and how bright You are and how tall You are, and I told them that You were taller than any human person and that You were taller than the entire whole universe, and they knew that, but they did not believe me. I said how I stayed with You for hundreds of years and that I cried for a lot of it, and it was a good crying, but they did not believe me. I told them how I saw Your Army of Angels and how there are more Angels than anyone could count in a million billion entire whole lifes, but they did not believe me. I told them how You sent me through time into the past to meet King Arthur, and how he knighted me, and how I had a mission to find the Holy Grail with Sir Ironside and Sir Ernest, and how You took my Mini Movie and made it a real thing for me. They did not believe me. I pray people believe me someday.

Nobody believes me.

They said I was dreaming.

I heard them say I was crazy.

I took lots of tests at the hospital. They stuck needles in my arms and took out my blood. They put me back in that machine where I was on my back and I had to be still for a long time and they said they were taking pictures of my brain. Doctor Hemming gave me blocks to play with in my hospital bed and asked me to make them fit, but I could not. He said it was okay. Doctor Hemming also said things to me and told me to say them back, but I could not remember. I think this is funny because I remember that my adventure happened, but I cannot remember what Doctor Hemming wanted me to say. I think this is because You give me the power to remember when I really need to. Doctor Hemming said it was okay that I did not remember, but he was sad. He looked at all these papers in his hands and I asked him what they were. He said they were tests. I asked him if I got a one hundred. He smiled and said it was not that kind of test. I asked him if he was sad because I failed. He said that he was not sad, and that I did not fail, but I did not believe him because he was lying. I got tired and asked if I could take a nap. He said that was okay. He said he was going outside in the hall to talk to Emily because he wanted to tell her how well I did. But he was lying. I knew I failed the tests.

I know because I saw them talk.

I did not like what I saw.

What I saw made me cry.

I was looking out the window and it was raining, but this is not what made me cry. That is because I could see two things. What I saw was the reflection in the rainy window. So I could see the rain outside, and also what was behind me in the hall. And in the reflection I saw Emily and Doctor Hemming in the hall. They were talking. Emily was shaking her head and looking down. I saw her look up. She was crying. She hugged Doctor Hemming. And Doctor Hemming hugged her. I did not see her face because her head was on his shoulder. But then she turned her head and put it on his other shoulder. I saw her face. Emily was still crying. That is why I cried. Because I love Emily and I did not want her to cry.

And I did not want to watch Emily cry. If you love someone, then you do not want them to cry. You also do not want to see them cry. You want to make it better. But I knew she was crying because I failed the tests. So I could not make it better. I wanted to go away because she would be better if I were not here. So I looked out the window at the rain and I prayed to You. I prayed she would never be sad again. I prayed I would go away so Emily would be happy.

God, You heard me.

I know You heard me.

You answered this prayer.

The door opened and there was sadness. Emily and Doctor Hemming both had sadness. Sometimes you can feel sadness in other people, sometimes you cannot. I could feel their sadness. They were trying to hide their sadness, but I still felt it. Emily tried hard not to show her sadness and she did not do a good job because she kept crying. Doctor Hemming held her hand while she talked. She told me I was sick. She said something had been happening to my brain since I died a long time ago and came back to life. She said it is a miracle I lived even one day after. She said that my brain is hurting me. She said I had many things wrong and she said many words that were long and hard to say but I do not remember them. I told her I had an adventure and she shook her head at me and said it was just a dream because my brain is bad. But I know my dream is true even if she does not believe me. She got real sad then and she cried hard, and it was all at once, and she told me that I was going to die in a few weeks and that maybe it would be sooner. She said that she could not take care of me anymore and that I had to go live at Morning Institute. I said it is called Morning Home, but Emily said that does not really matter right now. There was lots of sadness then. I did not want Emily and Doctor Hemming to have sadness. I had sadness too, but I did not cry. I also had madness, but I did not yell. I was also almost tricked into getting mad at You in my mind because something said I should be mad at You, but I was not mad. I did good. I only wanted to cry.

I prayed not to cry.

I prayed for them to leave.

I prayed to sleep and dream.

God, You heard me. I know because you answered this. Emily stopped talking. She asked if I wanted to listen to my music and I said yes. She said she had to go take care of things and I said okay. She told me to sleep and dream, and I said okay. She and Doctor Hemming left. I listened to my music and a good song came on. I was sad, but I was also happy. I was happy because You spoke to me by answering my prayer, so I fell asleep.

I had a good dream.

But this time it was just a dream.

I do not remember it.

Twenty-Three

THE UNFAIREST FIGHT

God, life is not fair.

Life is a fight.

But it is not a fair fight.

Life is the unfairest fight. I am not sad about it, but I am sad about it sometimes. I was sad earlier when I had to come here. I am at Morning Home now. I do not like it here. Emily brought me. Doctor Hemming and Pastor Nate were waiting for us when we got there. I came here in a wheelchair. I did not need a wheelchair at first, but then I did. When I got out of the car, we walked to the door but I got dizzy and my legs got heavy and I almost fell. I could not walk. Doctor Hemming held me up, and Pastor Nate got a wheelchair. Doctor Hemming said that my brain was having problems and that it would be on and off like a light switch, and that I should not get alarmed. I told him that I did not have any alarms except my alarm clock and I asked him if I should never set it. He laughed, but then he was sad and I could tell because he had a sad face. He told me that is not what he meant. He told me my brain was bad and he meant that things will happen where I will not be able to think right, or walk right, or do certain things with my body and I should not be afraid. I said I will fight my bad brain. He told me that I could not fight my brain. He said my name before he said this. When people say your name it means you are supposed to pay very close attention. He said, Todd, this is just not the kind of thing you fight. And I nodded my head to him and I said okay.

But it was not okay. I had lots of sadness and madness. I wanted to fight back. I thought this was unfair because something was hurting me and I was not allowed to fight it. A person should be allowed to fight back because that is fair. I had more sadness and madness and I wanted to cry, but I did not. If I cried it would just give other people sadness and madness. This gave me even more sadness and madness because I was in a hurt and I could not say anything. So I prayed in my mind for Your Help because You fight for people who cannot. You fight for people when things are unfair. Even if life is unfair, I know You are fair.

But I still felt bad.

I felt bad when we went inside.

Also when we got to my new room.

I felt bad because my new room was not like my room at home. There were bars on the windows. It smelled like when Emily mops the kitchen floor. Emily cried. But she stopped as soon as she started. She kept saying sorry. She had a box of my things. There were Superman comics, and X-Men comics also my Spider-Man comics, and the Calendar of Todd, and my mixtapes too. There was also my backpack. The book I stole for Izzy is in my backpack, but nobody knows. It is good because if Emily knew she might get mad. She would ask why I have it and maybe cry. I do not want that. She is sad now, but she will be happy soon. I will be out of her life. This is good. Doctor Hemming told me they would take care of me here. I said okay. Emily said I would get to see Izzy a lot because she was here too. Emily said she told Izzy that I would be here now. Emily asked if I was happy about Izzy being here too. And I was really happy I was near Izzy. But I still felt bad. I said okay, but lied. I was not okay.

I did not want to talk.

I wanted to be alone.

They would not let me be alone.

I told them to leave me alone. But they did not leave. They did not understand. Being alone does not mean being alone. I would be with Jesus Christ. That is not alone. Pastor Nate said he wanted to talk to me alone. I said okay but I did not care. Doctor Hemming got mad and said I did not need religious platatoods. I did not know what religious platatoods meant. Also I did not care.

Pastor Nate said okay and that he would pray for Doctor Hemming too. Doctor Hemming got mad and talked loud and said he did not need religion. Pastor Nate said nobody needs religion, but everybody needs Jesus. Doctor Hemming did not like that at all. Doctor Hemming is a good person, but he is angry. He is angry because he does not know You. I pray for him that he would know You. Anyone who does not know You is angry, God. That is because they do not know You are a hero. They do not know what is true and what is not. When a person knows that You are a hero and that You only want good things for them, they are not angry anymore. They become happy. Then they know You will never leave them. This makes me happy because I will never be alone.

I am happy too, but also afraid.

This is because I am confused. Everything is different. I am afraid because I do not know what day it is. I have lost track of my days. Emily said I can do it once I am settled, but I need to know what day it is and I told this to Emily. She said I will have to change The Calendar of Todd. I started crying. She asked me why I was crying. I told her it was because I never change The Calendar of Todd, but now I have to. So now I am confused and I do not like it.

I said, Emily I am confused.

She said, You're not confused.

I said, But I am.

She said, You're not confused, you're hurting. You're hurting because life is changing now and it's okay to feel this way.

I said okay but I was not okay. But God, I did understand then. I was not confused, I was hurting. This hurt is in my heart. It is a big hurt. I was in a big hurt because things were unfair.

Pastor Nate told Emily and Doctor Hemming to give him a minute with me so they left. Pastor Nate sat on my new bed. I did not need to sit because I was already in the wheelchair. We did not say anything to each other at first. It was weird. He asked if I understood what was happening. I said yes and I told him my brain was bad and I was going to die in a few weeks and maybe sooner and that is why I was here. He nodded his head up and down. He asked me if I was scared about this and I said no because I am going to Heaven when I die and

and I met Jesus Christ in person last night so it is okay. Pastor Nate nodded his head up and down again, but he did not believe me. Then I did not say anymore. He asked me if I was mad. I did not say anything. He said it was okay if I was mad. I still did not say anything. Then Pastor Nate asked if I was sad. I still did not say anything. He told me to look at him so I looked at him, but I did not say anything. He asked me if I was sad and I was sad, but I did not say anything because I would not say anything. I wanted to say that it was unfair I had to leave my home. It was unfair that I had to live at Morning Home. It was unfair that I could not walk right. It was unfair that my brain was not working right and it was unfair that I was going to die. But things have been unfair since I died a long time ago and came back dumb.

I am dying now.

But I am still alive.

It is always unfair.

So I prayed. I did not know what to pray so I just asked You for help. But I could not pray out loud, so I did this in my mind. But my mind was bad and there were too many bad voices. They said bad things and it made me sad because I knew You heard, God. I could not pray right. I think Pastor Nate saw my face. He asked me what was wrong. He asked me why I was crying. I told him I did not know I was crying but I suppose I am crying. He asked me again. I told him I was just trying to pray but I could not and I told him that I knew God heard the bad words in my head and I did not want Him to be mad. I told him that I was tired of life and I was sad because life is a fight, but it is not a fair fight. I said life was the unfairest fight of all. He nodded his head. He said life was unfair a lot of the time to a lot of people. He said life was unfair to me. Then he told me a Bible story. It was about the prophet Elisha. He said there was this one time when Elisha the prophet was surrounded by an army and Elisha had a servant who got scared. Then Elisha prayed to God and then Elisha and his servant saw the Army of God surrounding them. He told me that it may seem unfair, but with God on your side, it is unfair to your enemies, because they have no chance of winning. He said that even when I die, I will win, because I will be going to Heaven. And he said if I was having trouble praying, he would pray for me.

He said the only real way to win a fight is praying to Jesus Christ. He said this is something people like Doctor Hemming do not understand yet, but hopefully they will soon. So we prayed. We prayed a truth. Some prayers are a false. But this prayer was a truth. I know when things are a truth. Sometimes people pray things and it sounds real, but it is not real. Sometimes people pray and say lots of nice words, but it is not a truth. Sometimes people wave their arms and yell and stuff when they pray, but it is not a truth. Those people are liars. But this was a truth prayer because it had truth power. I know truth prayers because I just do. When a prayer is a truth prayer, God, it has power from You and then I can feel it in my bones. It is not my power, it is the Power of Jesus Christ.

    I heard music.

    It was special music.

    This was in my mind.

    Nobody else could hear this music. It was better music than I had ever heard before and this was the first time I had ever heard it. I believe this was You, God. And I believe it was the Angels making the music. So I moved my head after we prayed. Pastor Nate asked me what I was doing and I told him that I was listening to music in my mind. He asked me what kind of music, and I told him it was God music. He looked at me weird. Then he told me that when you sing to God, the devil flees. He said there is a verse that says, Make a joyful noise unto the Lord. I was going to do that out loud. But then Emily and Doctor Hemming came back. They were going home. Emily kissed my head and was trying not to cry. She said that she would be back to visit. Doctor Hemming told me I was going to be fine. Then Pastor Nate gave me a thumbs up. Then they all walked out of the door and they waved to me and they left me and I was alone.

    So I made a hum noise.

    I sang in my mind.

    And in my heart.

    The music was good. I was not afraid or sad. I was all alone, but I was also not alone. It was going to rain and I could tell because of the clouds. They were gray. I could see it through the bars on the windows. I was still not afraid or sad. Because I was singing. I sang the song that was already playing in my mind.

I made a joyful noise. You and Your Angels were there, all around me, You were protecting me. I could not see them, but I knew they were there. I remember when I saw them before and how they all had swords and shields and how Jesus Christ had fire in His eyes. I knew the devil had to run far away because I was making a joyful noise. There were other voices too. Most times when there are other voices they are bad, but this time these were good. It was like every voice that ever sang was singing with me, and the music played and I liked it a lot.

This is a good feeling.

Twenty-Four

KING TODD AND THE KNIGHTS OF THE SQUARE TABLE

God, I think I am a good friend.
You have also given me good friends.
My friends are cool.

I think many other people do not think they are cool. That is because one of my friends is mentally retarded and the other is a crazy person. I think people make fun of my friends and probably do not like us because they think we are weird, but we are not. That is because people like what is bad and hate what is good. The Bible says not to do that. The Bible says this, Hate what is evil and cling to what is good. I read this in Romans 12:9. But people only like a person if you are rich or good looking or can tell people what to do. I am not like that because I am not rich and I cannot tell people what to do and I am thirty-three but also seven so I am not good looking that way. My friends are also not rich, and they cannot tell anyone what to do, and they are not good looking that way either. My friends are cool though. But I think people think my friends are not cool because people cannot see goodness. I can see it. Goodness is easy to see, but sometimes you have to be careful because people are sometimes liars. I am dumb, but I am smart, and I knew when I met my friends that they had real goodness. It is like Jesus Christ. Some people do not think Jesus is cool because they do not know anything. If they did, they would love You. That is because they would see that Jesus Christ is cooler than all people. He is smart and funny. He is good and faithful. He is a healer. He is a warrior. God, it says so in the Bible.

In the Bible it says, The LORD your God is with you, the Mighty Warrior who saves. He will take great delight in you; in his love he will no longer rebuke you, but will rejoice over you with singing. This is from Zephaniah 3:17. It is a truth. That is why Jesus Christ is cool.

I forgot what I was saying.

God, I was in the Television Room with Ernie and Ira. Also, Ernie looks a lot like Sir Ernest and Ira looks a lot like Sir Ironside. I told them this and they both thought it was cool, and Ira says that he is from England, and Ernie said he is not from England but his mother used to tell him stories about knights. Maybe they both had grandparents long ago who were Sir Ernest and Sir Ironside. I told them this and they both thought it was cool. Ira asked if he could be a knight and then Ernie asked if he could be a knight too. I said yes, but I said I could not knight them because I am not a king, I am Todd and I am thirty-three but also seven. I felt bad about this because they wanted new names. When you get knighted, you get a new name. My friends have good names, but they just wanted better names.

My name is good.

I like my name.

But my name could be better too.

A king can give you a new name. When I go back in time inside my Mini Movie, my name is Sir Todd, Knight of the Morning. That is because King Arthur knighted me this. I said this to Ernie and Ira and they said there was a king who could knight them. I asked them who this king was. Ernie said he was sitting over there and pointed to the king of the television room. So we went over to the king. I do not like this person.

This king is fat.

This king is mean.

This king is not a good king.

I said, Hello, King of the Television Room, my name is Todd.

The King said that he would not speak with newbies. I asked what a newbie was because I did not know. Ernie got mad and pounded his fist on the table and told the King not to be mean to me. The King said that if we were not civil he would ban us from the television room. Then I said I do not know what civil is either. Ira told us to be quiet and just let him do the talking, and then Ira did some talking. Ira told the King we wanted new names and we wanted him to knight us so we could be knights.

The King said, That might be one of the dumbest thing I have ever heard. You know you live in a mental institution, right?

Ira told him that the king walked around in a sheet and fedora. The King did not like that and called Ira names that I cannot say because they are bad. Then Ira told the king we would not leave until he knighted us.

The King said, Do you know why you're here? Because you are broken, busted and messed up, a bunch of fools, and dorks and losers, that's what this place is for. Fools and dorks and losers. There's something wrong with all of you.

Ernie said, I have nothing wrong with me.

The King said, Everything is wrong with you, and you too and you too.

And the King pointed to me and Ira when he said that, so it was worse.

Ira said, Just knight us, man.

The King said, Fine. I knight you knights of whatever.

I said, You have to give us names and you have to call me Sir Todd.

He said, Fine, whatever. Sir Todd, Sir Ernie, Sir Ira, leave.

I said, You have to say we are knights of something.

Then he told us we were knights of the fools and dorks and losers. He smacked each of us on the forehead and said, Knighted.

We went back to our other table. It was not that fun. This king was mean. We were knights. But we did not feel like knights. The King made us feel like fools, dorks and losers. A good king makes his knights feel good. God, if I were a king, I would tell everyone how good they can be. I would make them feel good all the time. That is a truth. I would not say bad words about people. I would not make people feel bad about themselves. I would not smack them on the head. I would even try to make the bad people better. That is like You. In the Bible it says, Do not be overcome by evil, but overcome evil with good. This is from Romans 12:21. I said this verse to Ernie and Ira. They said it was a truth.

Ira said, Todd, you should be our king.

I said, But I am just Todd, I am not a king.

Ira said, Neither is the guy wearing a fedora and a sheet.

Ernie said, Be a king, Todd.

I said, What would I be king of?

Ernie said, You can be king of stories.

Ira said, That works.

Ernie yelled, King of stories.

Ira said, King of stories.

I said, What does the king of stories do?

Ira said, Well he tells stories.

Ernie said, I like your stories, Todd.

Ira said, Me too.

I said, Can the King of Stories make knights?

Ira said, Of course he can.

Ernie said, Todd, will you be King of Stories?

I said, Okay, first I have to make you knights.

So I asked them to please kneel. Ira and Ernie both kneeled. Everyone in the television room watched and they were quiet. Then I spoke loud. I said that I was the king of stories and I knight you. And I touched them both on the shoulder. Then Ernie whispered to me and told me not to forget to name them knights of something. I forgot that. I did not know what to say. And I saw the square table we were sitting at, so I said, You are both Knights of the Square Table. And I told them to stand up. They both stood up. Ira ruffled my hair. Then he slapped our hands. Everyone clapped for us. The nurses came in and told everyone to shut up. We did not care. If it meant we were fools, dorks and losers then I was happy to be one. I was a friend to others. And You made me a king.

My name was Todd, King of Stories.

Twenty-Five

A STORY FOR IZZY

God, I need another story.

I have been made King of Stories.

But You are the real King of Stories.

You have made all good stories. If I think about it, I am a story. Ernie is a story too. Ira is a story too. God, Izzy is also a story. All people are stories. You are a good storyteller. You also made the universe. That is a good story too. You also wrote the Bible and that is a good story. Some people do not like the Bible, but I think that is because they have never read it and because they are afraid to be wrong about life. There are bad stories too, but that is because people make bad choices. You have given me a good life because You just have, and because I also do what You say. You have made me a good story. But I need another story. I need it to help people. I think people just need a good story and it will help them with what they need help with. That is because in good stories there is goodness that helps people beat badness. I think stories filled with goodness are the best gifts. All good gifts are from God. That is in the Bible. In the Bible it says, Every good and perfect gift is from above, coming down from the Father of Heavenly Lights, who does not change like shifting shadows. That is from James 1:17. So I pray for a good gift from You to help Ernie, Ira and Izzy.

But what I really want is to help Izzy.

That is because she needs help. She came to me in the television room when I was watching television with Ernie and Ira. The King of the television room said he would let us watch whatever we wanted. We let Ernie pick. Ernie picked a cartoon, and it was He-Man and the Masters of The Universe. I used to watch this a long time ago, but I do not know when because I never wrote it down in the Calendar of Todd. We were watching this cartoon and there was no room on any of the chairs so I sat on the floor next to Ernie. Ernie knows every word to every He-Man cartoon and he says them while the cartoon plays. The cartoon was good, then it was over. But when it was over, the king of the television room turned on the news and it made him angry.

Then he broke the television.

The king of the television room threw his coffee mug at the television and it smashed the screen and then the screen broke. Then nobody said anything because nobody knew what to say. And when it was over I stood up and I saw Izzy there. She was standing near the doorway and she waved. She looked pretty today. She did not look like that time I was here when she did not talk. She was wearing ripped jeans and a pretty shirt. Her hair was not messy. She waved and I waved back and then I went to her. She gave me a hug and I hugged her back and I sat down next to her. I did this because my body was working okay today and I did not need a wheelchair. Then I told her all about my adventures and how I went to the movies by myself and how I went back in time to be a knight with King Arthur. She listened to me talk and I talked for a while. I told her how I had to go to the hospital after. She did not like that. I told her I was going to die because my brain was bad and she cried. I did not want to tell her, but I had to because you must be honest with people. I told her not to cry, but she cried. And she hugged me hard. I told her it was okay because God was writing me a good story. Izzy did not understand. But I told her that we all have stories.

Izzy has a story.

It is a sad story. And the ending is not done. I know because I read this story. I remembered it because I just do. Then I told Izzy I remember something.

She said, What do you remember?

I said, I stole your book back.

She said, You did what?

I said, I stole your book back from Morton the fat man.

She said, Where is it?

I said, It is here in my backpack.

And I opened up my backpack and I gave her the book. She got quiet. She looked at me and she was sad. I asked her why she was sad.

She said, I thought they took it. I thought they were going to throw it away. These are my memories, all my memories.

I said, That is why I wanted to get it back for you.

She said, You didn't read it did you?

I said, No I did not read your book, Izzy.

But this was a lie, God. So I asked You for forgiveness in my head. She was happy then. I think she has a good story coming. I pray this story comes true. I prayed for that where I was. And I tried to do it in my head but I could not think right. So I tried to do it out loud and talking, but I could not open my mouth. Izzy was asking me what was wrong, but I could not talk so I could not tell her what was wrong even though I wanted to.

And I could not move.

I could not even blink.

I could not do anything.

My head hurt, God. I was afraid. I fell over. I remember shaking. Izzy was standing over me screaming for someone to help me and I wanted to tell her it was okay but I could not. She rolled me on my side and I think I threw up a little bit or maybe a lot. I do not know. I got tired. I was falling asleep, so I prayed in my mind and this time I could pray in my head. I prayed for You to keep me safe while I sleep and dreamed. Sometimes I have bad dreams, so I prayed for good dreams. I did this right before I fell asleep.

But also I am not ready to die.

So I prayed another thing.

I prayed I would wake up.

Twenty-Six

A VISION FROM GOD TO TODD

I have hope.

My hope is to live.

You will make me live again.

One day I will die, but then I will live again. You promised this. So it is not wrong to hope for this. It is a truth. So I hope to live again *because dying is not fun*. I have been in bed all day. I fell asleep because I could not do anything. But now I am awake and I can move and talk again. But I am still in bed. I am tired. I will be dead soon. They told me I fell in the television room and went to sleep for an entire whole day. They said it was the fault of my brain and they thought I was dead. But I am not dead. I am alive. I am alive because You keep me alive. That is why I have hope to live again. Some people say they have hope, but they do not. They wish. They do not know hope. But I know hope. Hope is trusting in what is true. God, You are true, so I trust You. That is hope that cannot be taken. I trust in You because You are God and do not lie. You made the entire whole world, and also You made me. You became Jesus Christ and died for me and became alive again. God, I trust in You because You said that You love me and have saved me for eternal life. That is why I love You back. You do not lie. This is why I trust what You say. This is why I have hope when I die.

I am not afraid to die.

I am afraid, but I am not that afraid.

That is because I am never alone.

Sometimes I am alone. But You make me feel like I am not alone. All my life I have been alone. I am always alone. Even when I am with people, I am still alone. That is because I can never say what I mean to say because I do not know how to say it. Sometimes I can never even think what I want. It is like in X-Men when Professor X or Jean Grey or Cable gets hit in their minds by bad guys sending bad thoughts and then they cannot think right. I do not have powers like them. But I do have You. You know me, and I know You. You make me feel like I am not alone, even when I am alone.

You are also my best friend.

Best friends stay with each other.

They are never really alone.

I was alone when I woke up. But then I was not alone. That is because Ernie came to see me. He sat by my bed. He was glad I was alive and not dead. He gave me a hug. He said he prayed for me to be alive and I was alive so that was a good thing. Ernie asked me to tell him a story since I am the king of stories. I wanted to. But I was tired. I wanted to sleep. I could not move and talk good. But I told Ernie I would tell him a story. He asked me if he could invite friends. I said okay. Ernie got out of the chair and went into the hallway and he was out there talking to people. He came back into my room with lots of people. I do not know their names but I have seen them. They live here at Morning Home. They all sat down in my room and they waited for me to talk. Ernie said that he told them I was the king of stories and that I told good stories to my friends. Ernie said to me that everyone he brought wanted to be my friend. Ira was there too, and many other people. There was a lot of them. There was twenty people, but I am only saying that number because I did not count so I do not know the real number. It looked like a lot. Even the king of the television room was there because he wanted to hear a story. I made new friends.

But they all changed.

I saw who they really were.

They were children.

You changed my eyes, God. I could see something new. You showed me. They were a bunch of children, just like me. It happened when they walked into my room. It was like in movies when people go into new worlds and they go through doorways and things change, it was like that. Each person walked into my room and then became a child. They were themselves. But they were different. They were no longer big people, they were small. They were their true selfs.

I said, Ira, you are a small person.

Ira said, Todd, I'm two twenty and I got no fat on me, man.

But he was small. So was Ernie, and the others too. Then Izzy walked in and she changed too. She became a child and they all were the same size as me. We were all children. I said, You look like me, you are all children like me.

They laughed.

They did not get it. That is okay. Because we were all laughing. God, I think You did this. You did something to my eyes so I could see them for who they really were. I said this to all of them too, that it was because God did this. I told them also that God sent me back in time into my Mini Movies so I could tell them stories of my adventures. They were all interested and quiet and ready to listen. But I was tired. I did not want to talk. I told them I do not want to talk because I am tired. I said my brain was bad and I am tired. But then the king of the television room came close to me, and he looked at his feet and he was afraid to talk but he did talk and he said that maybe if we pray together, maybe God will give you power to tell a story to everyone. So I said okay.

That is when we all prayed together and it was a short truth prayer and I asked in my heart and with my mouth for You to help me tell a story. But I was still tired, and saying the prayer made me even more tired. I told my new friends I was tired. I said that God always knows what is best and maybe I am not supposed to tell a story right now. I said they should all leave until I can tell a story. But my new friends did not listen to me and they would not leave. So I said okay fine I will tell you all a story. And I started to tell the story about how I went to be a knight with King Arthur but I was too tired. So I told Ernie to get my book. He asked me what kind of book it was. And I pointed to the big book. I told him it was the book I am writing to You, God. I said it is called God and Todd. And Ernie got the book and I opened up to the right page. And I told Ernie to read it for me. He asked me what this was. I told him it is called a Mini Movie.

Ernie asked me what a Mini Movie was. And I told him it was a movie preview but I call them Mini Movies. Ernie said okay and that he would read it. But he started and could not do it, so Izzy said she would.

She held the book.

Everyone sat down on the floor.

Izzy read the story.

I closed my eyes as she read it. There was music like in a movie. There was bigness like in a movie. There was adventure like in a movie. I could see it in my mind. And I felt something too.

It felt like hope.

PRESENTING A MINI MOVIE EPISODE OF
THE ADVENTURES OF TODD

IN

TODD
and
THE AMERICAN FRONTIER

An American EPIC
Part I
A Mini Movie by Todd

written for the screen by Todd Carpenter on Saturday October 11th, 1997

OVER BLACK.

The projector rolls, the whirring noise precedes the visible film perforations on the celluloid, a standard beep and the screen brightens as someone speaks --

Trailer voice.

>   NARRATOR (V.O.)
>   In the Old West, when bad guys
>   ruled, and stuff was really hard,
>   a wandering hero went searching.

THE AMERICAN FRONTIER.

A magnificent vista of western geography with rolling hills, snow peaked mountains. At the top of this grassy crest --

TODD.

Seven-years-old **riding a white horse.** Todd wears old west attire, outfitted in a cowboy hat, boots, jacket, jeans. For a weapon, a slingshot in his back pocket. A piece of long grass hangs in his mouth. He looks to the far horizon and pauses, gazing thoughtfully at the sun.

>   NARRATOR (V.O.)
>   Searching for purpose.

He pets the horse. The horse neighs. Todd gives the animal a light kick, they trot down the hill.

A RIVER BASIN.

Todd bends at the water with a pan, prospecting, sifting through rocks and loose surface sediment looking for gold. The white horse stands nearby.

>   NARRATOR (V.O.)
>   Searching for prosperity.

THE GREAT PLAINS.

Todd at dusk, sitting at his campfire. A small tent in the background, and fields for miles in every direction. The white horse rests its head on Todd's shoulder. Todd pets the horse, the sun setting in front of him.

>   NARRATOR (V.O.)
>   Searching for a home.

MOUNTAIN RANGE.

Todd rides his white horse slow on a makeshift path of rough terrain, navigating pine trees in the Colorado territory.

> NARRATOR (V.O.)
> Searching for the American Dream.

Todd stops his horse.

> NARRATOR (V.O.)
> When he found something else.

He spots something in front of him. He hops off the horse. The boy bends low and picks up a diary. He wipes dirt off it and opens it mid-way to -- **A MAP**.

> NARRATOR (V.O.)
> Adventure.

> TODD
> Horse, this is a map of something.

> NARRATOR (V.O.)
> A map of buried treasure.

> TODD
> This is a map of buried treasure.

> NARRATOR (V.O.)
> Written by a proper lady going by the name of Izzy.

> TODD
> It's written by a proper lady who goes by the name of Izzy. Horse, we will have to find the treasure and return it to this fair woman.

KA-CLACK -- the noise comes from behind Todd -- a dirty, EVIL COWBOY who looks a lot like Morton aims a shotgun at Todd.

> EVIL COWBOY
> That treasure belongs to the army of Outlaw Evil Bad Guy Cowboys.

> TODD
> This treasure belongs to a fair and proper lady named Izzy.

In one deft movement, Todd whips out the slingshot in his back pocket, aims, and FIRES a rock between the eyes of EVIL COWBOY, who falls over screaming in pain --

THE RIVER BASIN.

Todd rides on his white horse, fast, outrunning EVIL COWBOY and **ONE HUNDRED OTHER BAD COWBOYS** as they fire guns. Bullets graze Todd as he rides into dense trees.

> NARRATOR (V.O.)
> Now he must outwit the army of
> Outlaw Evil Bad Guy Cowboys.

THE HIGH PLAINS.

Todd at a campfire again at dusk, studying the diary.
The white horse rests its head on Todd's shoulder once more.

> NARRATOR (V.O.)
> He must decipher the map.

> TODD
> I must decipher this map.

> NARRATOR (V.O.)
> And find the buried treasure.

> TODD
> And find the buried treasure.

> NARRATOR (V.O.)
> And unite an army to fight this
> other army of outlaw Evil Bad Guy
> Cowboys.

> TODD
> I'll need to unite an army to fight
> this other army of outlaw Evil Bad
> Guy Cowboys.

> NARRATOR (V.O.)
> Also he must name his horse.

> TODD
> Also I must name you, horse.

Thunder in the sky -- it catches Todd's attention.

> TODD
> I'll call you -- **Thunder Son.**

The horse neighs again in agreement.

DESERT PLAINS.

Todd on Thunder Son in the middle of the day, riding fast with CANYONS in the background -- **blam-blam-blam** -- chased by the army of Outlaw Evil Bad Guy Cowboys firing at Todd.

> NARRATOR (V.O.)
> Can he escape the lawless west?

AN OPEN PRAIRIE.

Todd riding on Thunder Son approaching hundreds of NATIVE AMERICANS, three tribes at a standstill.

> NARRATOR (V.O.)
> Can he unite the Native Americans
> of the American territories?

UTAH.

Todd rides Thunder Son alongside an army of Native Americans in a desert terrain, approaching a canyon and --

A CAVE ENTRANCE.

Todd stops.

> NARRATOR (V.O.)
> Can he find the hidden treasure?

Rumbling.

Galloping.

It comes from behind Todd. He turns to face the other direction -- THE ARMY OF OUTLAW EVIL BAD GUY COWBOYS -- riding toward Todd and his army of Native Americans.

> NARRATOR (V.O.)
> Can he defeat the army of Outlaw
> Evil Bad Guy Cowboys? Find out
> this summer.

Todd readies his slingshot.

CUT TO BLACK.

> NARRATOR (V.O.)
> The Adventures of Todd:
> Todd and the American Frontier:
> An American Epic:
> Part One. Rated PG thirteen.

TODD AND THE AMERICAN FRONTIER

FOREVERLAND ENTERTAINMENT PRESENTS
A FOREVERLAND ENTERTAINMENT PRODUCTION "TODD AND THE AMERICAN FRONTIER" A TODD CARPENTER MINI MOVIE
STARRING TODD CARPENTER THUNDER SON EVIL COWBOY OUTLAW EVIL BAD GUY COWBOYS ARMY OF NATIVE AMERICANS
DESIGN BY TODD
DISTRIBUTED BY FOREVERLAND ENTERTAINMENT

Twenty-Seven

FREE
RAIN

God, tonight is Movie Night.

Movie nights are my favorite.

People here think I make movies.

I cannot make movies. I told them this, but nobody believed me. They said I could because they saw it in their minds. I saw it too, but it was all in my head and it was in their heads too. It was a Mini Movie I wrote many years ago. It was an adventure in the past. They saw me go be in the old west. They saw everything and they loved it. After it was done they asked me to do it again, but I could not. I told them I had other Mini Movies that I wrote from long ago when I was Body Seven and smart, and that I could not find them. But that was a lie. I have found another Mini Movie. And I am sorry for lying, but I am also not because I cannot show anyone. It is my last Mini Movie. And I do not know who wrote it. I do not think it was me and I do not remember writing it but I also do not remember many things anymore. So I said I could not find it. Then I was tired so I asked them to go. Now it is the next day and tonight is Movie Night.

We are supposed to watch a movie.

But we cannot. Our television is broke. God, my brain is broke too. It is all swirly in my mind. I am forgetting lots of things. I forgot what I said. Hold on. I have to look at what I wrote because I do not remember. Okay, I remember now. I said we are supposed to watch a movie. Our television is broke. We cannot have movie night because the king of the television room broke the television and it was broken in pieces and I saw it happen. I prayed for You to fix it. I do not remember if I told You, God. The King of the television room was watching the news and someone was being mean on television and he got mad. Then the King of the television room held his coffee cup and he threw it at the television screen and then it broke. And tonight is Movie Night. It is not Movie Night yet. It is daytime now. Movie Night is later, but it feels like night because I am tired.

I forgot what I said.

Now I remember. Our television is broken and tonight is Movie Night. So I prayed for You to fix it. I did not know what to pray for, so I asked for You to help. After I prayed, Ernie and Ira helped me in my wheelchair. God, my body is bad right now and I am using a wheelchair today because I am tired. Maybe not tomorrow. But Ernie and Ira brought me to the television room that does not have a television anymore. I felt okay but I am tired so much now. I do not know what day it is. I have not been writing down my days in the Calendar of Todd.

My brain is swirly.

They are making me take pills.

It is all swirly.

I am sorry. I am trying to remember, but it is weird in my head. It is like I am walking in a cloud and I am slow. Also, Pastor Nate showed up. He says he will come to Morning Home more since I am living here. He talked with us. Ernie and Ira did a lot of talking. I did not talk much. I could talk, but I did not. It was hard and made me tired. That is why I did not talk, even though I wanted to talk. I did talk when Pastor Nate asked me a question. He asked me if I was looking forward to Movie Night. I did not know then it was Movie Night. I love Movie Nights. Me and Emily had Movie Nights a lot. I told him I love Movie Nights and that is a truth. But Ira told Pastor Nate it would not happen because the television is broken. Then I got sad in my heart and in my mind. I kept my sadness in my heart and mind. When I am sad, I try hard to not ever say anything to anyone ever. Because I do not want my sadness to leak out to make other people sad. That would be bad. Then there would be double sadness. I think Pastor Nate knew I was sad because he looked at me and then he said he had an idea. Pastor Nate said he was going out for a minute and told us to hold tight.

That is when we waited.

We waited for a long time. I did not do anything at all because I was tired. But I had my friends. I watched Ernie and Ira play chess together. Except Ernie does not know how to play chess so they played it like checkers. Izzy was there too and she stayed with me. She asked if she could read to me. I said okay but told her I was afraid to sleep. She asked me why and I told her I was afraid to not wake up. She did not speak then. I told her it will be soon. She said it was okay and that I should rest.

And she went into my backpack and found a book to read. I know the book because Izzy used to read this book to me a lot and I read it many times when I was Body Seven and smart. It was Peter Pan by a person named J.M. Barrie. She asked me if I remembered it. I wanted to say I remembered it, and some parts I did remember and some parts I did not. One part I remember is when Peter Pan is on the rocks in the ocean and he is afraid and then he says he is ready to die. This is the same as me. But I did not tell Izzy this because she would get sad. So I said to her that I did not remember it. She said it was okay, and she started to read. I wanted to say something, but I fell asleep.

Then I woke up and it was dark out.

I was in my wheelchair and Izzy was near me, and so was Ernie and Ira. We were in the room with the broken television. When I woke up is when Pastor Nate finally returned to us. But this time Pastor Nate brought someone with him. His name was James. He said he remembered me very well. I told him I did not know him, but he said I did, and that I just could not remember. He said we met years ago. He said I used to go to his movie theater when I was seven years old.

I said, I am still seven.

This made him laugh. He said I used to go with Emily and we would go every Saturday and also Izzy sometimes. This is a truth. Then I remembered he owns the movie theater that shut down. It is the one I went where You took me. I did not tell him because he would not understand. So I said I remembered the theater. Because I did remember. I told him that the theater was shut down and nobody was there anymore. He said that the police called him after they found me at the theater, and it gave him an idea to reopen it. James said that he came here tonight to invite everyone to his reopening. He said he would reopen in a few days. And also, he wanted to show us a movie. I asked how he would do that because the television is broken. That is when he showed me his old movie projector. It was cool. He turned it on quick. The light flickered and shined and we were all quiet. Then he shut it off. He said he had a talk with Pastor Nate earlier. He said Pastor Nate told him our television was broken. So James brought us his film projector and movies to watch. James said that he wanted to show a movie here to all of us with the projector and that I could pick out the movie. Then James showed me all the movies he brought. They were in big circles that he called reals. I said but it is a movie not real. He said no, reals spelled r-e-e-l-s. I did not understand. He said that he brought them all for us. He asked me what my favorite movie was and I said that my favorite movie was Star Wars. I told him that the one I liked the best was with Yoda. That one is called The Empire Strikes Back. James said he had this movie. I said I liked it the best because in it Yoda says we are luminous beings. Yoda is not God, but he is right, because we are luminous beings.

Luminous means shiny bright.

We are shiny bright beings.

That is how God made us.

Then James said there was time for two movies. He asked me to pick another movie. I said that Izzy and Ernie and Ira could pick the next movie. They picked The Shawshank Redemption. Pastor Nate turned my wheelchair toward the white wall. Everybody else sat down too.

Then the lights turned down.

And there one was one light behind us.

It showed a picture on the wall.

It was a movie. And the movie was Star Wars. But I fell asleep. I was tired. I woke up at the good parts. Then the movie stopped. Then everybody took a break. And then we all came together again to watch the next movie. Then James turned on The Shawshank Redemption. I did not stay awake for this movie either. But I remember it and I got to see the end. The person in the movie has gotten unfariness and is in prison for his entire whole life. But he breaks out with a small hammer. He did it little by little. He broke out and got in a tunnel and climbed out and went toward the light and he found his way out. My face felt warm when I saw this, God. My eyes could not see, so I wiped them. There was water in them. I guess I was crying but I did not know I was until I found out that I was. And then I was crying a lot. I felt good for the person. He was free. I want to be free too. I pretended I was in the movie. That is why I cried.

    I cried when I got to my room. Crying made me tired. But I did not sleep. It is a funny thing, God. Sometimes you can be tired all day, and then be awake all night. When this happens you think many thoughts you do not want to think. I thought about my entire whole life. I thought about how I was smart once and how when I was Body Seven and smart that I wanted to be an astronaut. I wanted to make lots of money and be important and take care of Emily. I never did that. I did not make lots of money. I did not go to space except in my dreams. These were the thoughts that I thought. There are many things I did not do. I did not do them because I could not, but not because I did not want to. And I did not become an important person. But maybe I was important to someone.

    Then I heard something.

    I heard stones on my window. It was not stones, it was rain. I stopped thinking sad thoughts and got up and went to the window. I did not need the wheelchair then. I stood for a long time at the window. It was nice because I could stand on my own. I was thinking about The Shawshank Redemption. I felt like the guy in the movie. He was in prison. I feel like I am too. I even have bars on my windows. It makes me tired and want to give up. When you are tired, that is when you want to give up. I think that is what the world is. A prison that makes people give up. But You said You came to free the captives. You said it God, so it is true.

    The rain is free. It goes down from the clouds, but sometimes it goes sideways, and otherways and wherever it wants if the wind blows just right. Also Emily told me one time something I remember. She said the rain falls and then it changes into gas, and then the clouds suck water back up and it rains again and it happens over and over. That is what I thought when I watched the free rain. Soon I will fall like the rain. And soon I will go back to the clouds with You.

    Soon I will be free like the rain.

Twenty-Eight

A VISIT FROM THE DOCTOR

God, You are like a doctor.
You heal people and their hurts.
This is a good feeling.

But I did not have a good feeling today. I had sadness. I had too much sadness. I was in my room with sadness because I was alone. I was not really alone because You are always with me. But I still had sadness. I remembered I have not seen Emily for a long time. Emily does not come see me. She has not seen me since I got here. This is okay. It is better. I prayed for this. I do not remember much, but I remember that. I prayed that Emily would be away from me so she could be free. I do not want her near me. She would be sad. That is why I am sad. Because I prayed for a thing and it was a good thing, but it is sad. Sometimes you have to do that. Sometimes you have to be sad for others to be happy. It is not a good thing, but it is not a bad thing. It can be a happy thing.

I decided then to be happy.
Even though I had sadness.
I had happiness mixed with sadness.

So I decided to do another happy thing. I decided to read a comic book. I got my comics out of my bag. This comic was X-Men. I like X-Men a lot. God, in X-Men, the X-Men are people with powers, and the people of the world hate the X-Men. So the people of the world are always mean and trying to kill the X-Men. But even though the people of the world hate the X-Men and are always trying to kill them, the X-Men always protect the people anyway. I think that is kind of what it is like to be a follower of Jesus Christ. Because You said that we are supposed to love everybody, even our enemies who hate us. This is what the X-Men do. They protect and care for the people who hate them. I think it is cool and it is why I like X-Men. Also because it is a comic book and I like comic books. I like comic books because it is hard for me to read. I could not read the words when I was reading my comic. But I could see the pictures, and it was good.

Then there was a knock and I looked up.

It was Doctor Hemming at my door. He was in my new room. I asked why he was here and he said that he came to see how I was doing. Doctor Hemming said he missed our regular visits. I asked him if he was going to run some tests, and I also said that would be hard because we are not in his office.

Doctor Hemming said, No tests today.

I said, Did you bring the blocks?

He said, There won't be any more blocks, Todd.

But I knew that. I did not say that I knew though, because that would make things sad. I will be dead soon. Tests do not matter anymore. Then me and him did not say anything and it was quiet and weird. It made me feel weird because it was weird. Then I told Doctor Hemming I was going to the movies tomorrow. He asked me how I was going to the movies. I told him I am going to the old movie theater because the guy who owns it is reopening and invited me.

He said, That sounds like a fun Saturday.

Then I said, If tomorrow is Saturday then it is a White Day Saturday, and Emily and me always go to the movies on White Day Saturdays, except twice, and now we do not go anymore because I live here. Do you think she will go tomorrow? Doctor Hemming said he did not think Emily knew about this new trip. I did not say anything because I did not know what to say. But it would be nice if things were like White Day Saturdays again. Emily and me could go to the movies like before. I would like to do this again before I die. So I prayed to live a few more days, and I said I was praying to live a few more days.

Doctor Hemming did not know what to say.

He said, I don't know what to say.

I said, Why do you not know what to say?

He said, You're so aware of what's happening, and you're happy still.

I said, Because God is taking me to Heaven.

When I said that he did not talk for a bit and it was weird again. Then he said this is why he wanted to talk to me because there was not much time left. He said he wanted to ask me a sensitive question but this made no truth to me so I said, How are questions sensitive? Can questions feel? Then he said no, and that he wanted to ask an important question. I said okay. Then he talked about Emily and how much he cares about her. That was nice. But it was hard to pay attention, and I did not. But then I did because I could tell he was ready to finally say his important question.

He said, Here is my important question. I'm asking Emily to marry me.

That made me happy, God. I did not know what to say so I said, You should. Doctor Hemming laughed. Then I remembered. I remembered I prayed for this. I prayed Emily and Doctor Hemming would get married. So I got up and went to my bag and I got the Calendar of Todd. I flipped many pages, but I did not see my prayer. He asked me what I was doing and I said I was looking for my prayer. And I flipped and flipped all the pages. I did not remember where I wrote it but if it was important, I would have wrote it. Then I found something in blue. It was my prayer in big blue marker in a big blue circle. I showed him and said, Look, I prayed for you to marry Emily and now you are.

He said, Right, that's nice. I don't know if she'll say yes.

I said, She will say yes because she loves you.

He said, Well, I wanted to get your, you know, blessing.

I said, I cannot bless because I am not God.

He said, Todd, I'm just asking if you approve. Do you understand?

I said, I approve. And now you and me will pray together to thank God.

He said, Todd, no offense, that kind of thing is just not for me.

I said, Prayer is for everybody. It is just talking with God.

He said, I'm not sure I even believe in God.

I said, But why is that?

He said, It's complicated.

And I did not say anything, but I knew what Doctor Hemming wanted to say to me. Doctor Hemming wanted to say he did not believe in You because his family was killed and many bad things happened. I did not say this because Doctor Hemming would not understand, but I think that is a dumb reason, God. You are always there when the bad things happen and You help also. People do not get it. They do not understand that You do not make bad things happen to good people just to make them sad. People just do not get that sometimes bad things happen, and You always know when they happen, and when they are in a hurt that You hurt too, and You always can make it better, even when people die. All they need to do is trust You. So then I said something good, God. It is one of the best things I ever said and I am happy with myself for saying it.

I said, Sometimes bad things happen to good people, and sometimes good things happen to bad people, but sometimes good things happen to good people too, we do not know why, but God does. He will make it right in the end.

He said, I believed in God once.

I said, I know because I saw you yelling at Pastor Nate.

He laughed and nodded his head. Then I said, I know why you are mad. I know what happened to your family but they can never be hurt again because they are safe with God now.

He said, Are they?

I said, Yes. Also you cannot be an untruster in God if you already trusted Him before. And I think You trust in God. I think You are just mad at Him.

He was quiet and he did not say anything for a few seconds.

Then he said, Yes, I am mad.

Then there was quiet and then I said, Do you want to keep being mad?

He did not say anything. And then he turned his head away from me. He was crying, but not making any noise. I saw him wipe his eyes and he would not look at me. He was in a hurt.

He said, I don't want to be mad anymore, Todd.

Then I remembered a verse, God. You keep track of all our tears. I know this because in the Bible it says, You keep track of all my sorrows. You have collected all my tears in your bottle. You have recorded each one in your book.

This is from Psalm 56:8. Sorrows mean sadness and also tears. Pastor Nate told me this once. And then I remembered another verse. The Bible says You turn to me because You hear my cry. That one is from Psalm 40:1. I was real good at remembering verses today. So I told this to Doctor Hemming. I said that God cares about his tears, and that God will turn to him and hear his cry because that is in the Bible too. Then I asked if he wanted to pray. He did not say yes but he nodded his head. I did not know what to pray so I opened up my Bible to that verse in Psalm 40. It had to be this one, but I do not know why. I think You told me to. So I said I was going to pray this to him and he nodded his head again. He closed his eyes and I read the verse. Then we stayed like that and we were quiet and nobody said any words. I was praying, but I was doing this in my mind, and still we did not say any words. And then he cried. He did not make any sounds but he had tears on his face, so he was crying. Pastor Nate told me once that crying is a prayer and we do not have to say perfect words, God knows us. I think that is the kind of praying Doctor Hemming was doing.

    We prayed.

    I knew Doctor Hemming meant it.

    This is a good feeling.

Twenty-Nine

THIS
I
KNOW

God, this will be my last sleep.

This I know.

It is a sad feeling.

Tomorrow when I wake up, it will be my last day here. I do not know how I know this, but this I know. I am going to die soon, so I have some more prayers. I pray that tomorrow I do what You want me to do. I do not know what it is yet, but I know it is important. I pray You give me a good sleep so I am rested and strong. Tomorrow will be hard. I do not know how I know, but this I know. I have many prayers to pray, God. I have so many prayers that I forget what they are. I have so many prayers and no more time to pray them, and that is because sometimes I forget what I need to pray. So I will pray three prayers. My first prayer is that You please forgive me for all my sins, and I know You have, but I do not think it is bad to say again because I am making sure. My next prayer is for You to bless Emily and Doctor Hemming, and Pastor Nate, and Izzy and Ernie and Ira and give them whatever they want. My last prayer is this, I pray for all the people I love to be healed if they need to be healed, and not only of outside hurts, but inside hurts too, and for them to know You can do anything and You can do it big. And also if they do not know You, Jesus Christ, that they would.

I am glad I made that my last prayer.

I wish I could live to see it.

This is a sad feeling.

PRESENTING A MINI MOVIE EPISODE OF
THE ADVENTURES OF TODD

IN

GOD
and
Todd:
THE MOVIE

A cool funny sad but also happy EPIC
A Mini Movie by Todd

written for the screen by Todd Carpenter on Sunday November 1st, 1998

This is my best Mini Movie which I wrote Saturday night because I saw it in my dream and I woke up and I wrote it and finished at 11:59 at night but now it is 12:00 so now it is Sunday good night.

TODD'S MOVIE LOGO.

A mountainous peak in the distance with an ice capped summit. At the top of the summit stands a seven-year-old boy in jeans and a t-shirt and a baseball cap, holding the AMERICAN FLAG. He waves to the camera and plants that flag, overshadowed by the background sound of a bus braking and opening its door --

>   TODD (V.O.)
> Hello, my name is Todd. I am thirty-three years old but I am also seven. People think this is strange, and I guess it is, but I do not think this is strange.

STREET CORNER BUS STOP.

Seven-year-old Todd (who always looks seven and never a mentally handicapped thirty-three year old) stands at the corner of his street, in front of an open bus door. Todd speaks to ROGER, fifty, the bus driver, haggard hair, gaunt, smoking a cigarette, staring back at Todd, perplexed.

>   TODD
> My favorite things are comic books and movies and superheroes and Star Wars and King Arthur.
>
>   ROGER
> Right.
>
>   TODD
> I also like watching movies and I also like listening to Bruce Springsteen and also sneakers are cool and horses too.

Roger continues staring at Todd.

>   ROGER
> You getting on this bus, son?
>
>   TODD
> Okay.

Roger motions Todd to get on the bus. Todd does so.

>   NARRATOR (V.O.)
> Meet Todd.

TODD.

His room. Posters of movies on the wall, toy action figurines on shelves, comics and clothes strewn on the floor.

Todd --

Standing in front of his closet mirror. **For this moment only** Todd has the physical appearance of a thirty-three year old, but the mirror image portrays something else --

A seven-year-old.

This is how Todd sees himself.

He waves to the reflection.

THE BUS.

Seven-year-old Todd in a window seat. He looks out the window at his small town in upstate New York as the bus drives down the main street: little shops, the main grocery store, the bank. Morning is a special corner of small-town America.

> NARRATOR (V.O.)
> Todd lives in Morning, New York.

> TODD (V.O.)
> I live in Morning, New York and I
> have lived in Morning, New York my
> entire whole life and also I will
> live in Morning, New York the rest
> of my entire whole life.

EMILY.

Driving her sedan circa 2008, Todd sits in the passenger seat. Emily wears scrubs, a forty-three year old nurse with long messy hair.

> NARRATOR (V.O.)
> Todd has a sister.

> TODD (V.O.)
> I have a sister. Her name is Emily.
> She is always happy except for when
> she is not, which is a lot.

Todd puts a mixtape into the old car's tape deck player. Emily ejects it before it plays.

                    EMILY
          I don't want to listen this
          eighties crap right now.

                    TODD
          Why?

                    EMILY
          Because I don't.

                    TODD
          Why?

                    EMILY
          Because I just don't.

                    TODD
          Why?

                    EMILY
          I just don't want to listen to it,
          okay?

                    TODD
          Why?

                    EMILY
          Why do you keep asking why?

                    TODD
          Because I want to know why.

                    EMILY
          Because I don't.

Silence between them for a moment.

                    TODD
          Why?

She groans an exhausted sigh.

THE TELEVISION ROOM.

At Morning Home, a mental institution. White bland walls, and all manner of troubled individuals occupy this room, many in sweat pants and t-shirts or hospital gowns.

Except for --

IRA, a six foot, muscular, two-hundred and twenty pound, thirty-three year old half-white half-black man who looks rather intellectual with his glasses. He ruffles Todd's hair and gives Todd a pat on the back.

ERNIE, also thirty-three, diminutive, suffering from down syndrome, but smiling and running over to Todd for a hug.

>   NARRATOR (V.O.)
>   Todd has friends.

>   TODD (V.O.)
>   My friends are Ira and Ernie and --

IZZY. Dark haired and lithe, beautiful and sad. She wears sweat pants, sitting on the couch in this room with a medicated, blank stare at the television.

>   TODD (V.O.)
>   Izzy. I love Izzy. We are like
>   Peter Pan and Wendy.

Todd looks at the guards, THREE MEN armed with batons, and MORTON, a fat little man with a cynical face.

>   TODD (V.O.)
>   But all my friends are prisoners.

TODD.

Now at the old, boarded up movie theater at night.
One lone streetlight shines above him and -- IT POPS.

Darkness.

The wind blows.

Todd shivers. The night becomes even darker, blotting out the sky and the stars and with it. Voices in the background. Indistinct whispers of wickedness, but all that can be discerned from them is sibilant slurring.

The streetlight GLOWS, this time without a bulb, and this time the shining light emits an otherworldly illumination, warm and protective and **BRIGHT**, surrounding Todd and outlining a path for him straight to -- **THE MOVIE THEATER**.

>   NARRATOR (V.O.)
>   And Todd has a purpose.

Todd walks forward to the the boarded up theater.
He cuts right through the darkness and the evil whispers, he opens the doors to the theater and --

THE SECRET PLACE.

All white everything. A shining bright floor, mirror like, and an even brighter light in front of him in the ambiguous outline of a person. Todd approaches. Sound reverberates around him in a powerful whisper, gentle and kind --

     GOD
  Set them free.

     TODD
  Set who free?

The light floods the screen as an inspirational film score plays in the background gearing up for its final movements --

TODD.

In a hospital bed. Alone, asleep. An IV in his arm. At his bedside, Emily and DOCTOR HEMMING speak low.

     DOCTOR HEMMING
  He only has a few weeks left.
  Maybe even days.

Todd opens one eye, feigning sleep.

     NARRATOR (V.O.)
  Now he must discover that purpose,
  and succeed in his mission, before
  it's too late.

HOSPITAL ENTRANCE.

Little seven-year-old Todd walks out the sliding doors, now in his jeans and T-shirt, still with the IV in his arm.

     NARRATOR (V.O.)
  Todd Pictures presents a film
  starring Todd Carpenter --

IZZY.

Smiling in a rare moment in the Morning mental institution. She reads Peter Pan to Todd, who lays in bed.

     NARRATOR (V.O.)
  Izzy Eaton --

ERNIE AND IRA.

Ira tussling Todd's hair while Todd smiles. Ernie puts his arm around Todd and brings him in for a big hug.

          NARRATOR (V.O.)
  Ernie and Ira --

EMILY.

On the back porch at night with Todd, both of them looking at the stars. She holds Todd's hand and smiles at him.

          NARRATOR (V.O.)
  And Emily Carpenter.

          TODD
  What is my purpose, Emily?

          EMILY
  It will find you. That's life.

HOSPITAL ENTRANCE.

Todd rips the IV out of his arm. The wind rustles, and in the air the gentle whisper returns --

          TODD
  Where do I go?

          GOD
  This way.

          NARRATOR (V.O.)
  A film by Todd Carpenter

With a determined face, Todd RUNS -- he SPRINTS -- and a symphony hits its high thirty second crescendo in a full orchestra, with Todd running the way people run in epic and uplifting movies alongside an epic and uplifting score reminiscent of 1990's era cinema while the song continues --

The screen flashes to --

THUNDER SON THE STARFIGHTER.

Todd in the cockpit, maneuvering the steering stick and firing lasers out at enemy alien ships in space --

                        CUT TO:

TODD.

Riding THUNDER SON the horse at near light speed through his small town, riding *so fast that the background becomes all white* like shooting stars flaring behind him --

                                            CUT TO:

THE MEDIEVAL ENGLAND COUNTRYSIDE.

Todd running over a grassy hill holding Excalibur, this time beside THUNDER SON, Sir Ironside and Sir Ernest as they charge reckless into a horde of GOBLINS --

                                            CUT TO:

UTAH DESERT.

Todd once again riding THUNDER SON, now in the old west, in the middle of a war with THE ARMY OF OUTLAW EVIL BAD GUY COWBOYS -- Todd aims his slingshot at an Evil Cowboy --

                                            CUT TO:

TODD.

At sunset, in the cornfield in Morning, New York.
The symphony marks its denouement in conjunction with Todd watching the sun on the horizon, setting low and red.

             NARRATOR (V.O.)
        The world will never be the same
        once you've seen it through the
        mind of God...and Todd.

             TODD
        Hoping is my favorite thing.
        So I always hope with you, God.
        This is a good feeling.

And so the sun sets as Todd watches with a smile, awaiting wonderful things to come.

                                            FADE TO BLACK.

GOD and Todd: THE MOVIE

FOREVERLAND ENTERTAINMENT PRESENTS
A FOREVERLAND ENTERTAINMENT PRODUCTION "GOD AND TODD: THE MOVIE" A TODD CARPENTER MINI MOVIE
STARRING GOD TODD CARPENTER EMILY CARPENTER IZZY EATON ERNIE & IRA DOCTOR HEMMING PASTOR NATE
DESIGN BY TODD
DISTRIBUTED BY FOREVERLAND ENTERTAINMENT

Thirty

THE LAST DAY

God, today is my last day.

It is also movie day.

This is a sad day but a nice day.

It is sad because I have to say goodbye. It is nice because I know I am going to Heaven. That is good. That is why You woke me up early. Then I prayed and my prayer was good. I did not have bad thoughts. I said thank You for waking me up. Then I prayed for Your Help today. I always pray for Your Help, but I really need it now because I have to do things today which make me sad. In my prayer I heard You tell me to do some things. I heard it in my heart. You told me to write them down so I did. God, here are the things You told me to do.

1. Write a goodbye note to your friends
2. Tell Izzy to escape
3. Tell Emily she did a good job
4. Forgive yourself
5. Come home

God, I saw the list and some things I did understand and some things I did not understand. I did not know why I should write a goodbye note because I am not going anywhere. The only place I am going is to the movies because today is movie day. It is also my last day. Then I understood. I am going to Heaven. So I put all my things in my backpack except this book to You. I am not done with this book called God and Todd, but soon I will be. But everything else I put in my backpack and then I wrote a note and the note said this.

> Hello. When I die, please give all my comics to Ernie and give my mixtapes to Ira. Please give my Peter Pan book and my Luke Skywalker toy to Izzy. Please give this book to Emily. I will miss you all because I love you. Please do not be sad. I will be happy soon. I am going to be in Heaven with God where I will be a luminous being forever. Goodbye.
> - Also this note is from Todd

This was hard to write. It was not hard to write with my hand. This was hard to write with my heart. It was hard to write because I do not want to go. Because I will miss Emily, and Ernie, and Ira, and Izzy, and Pastor Nate, and Doctor Hemming. But also I want to go because it will be good in Heaven. I am sick of Earth. I do not like it here anymore. I am sick of being dumb. I am sick of not being able to say what I mean because I am not smart enough to know the words. And I am sick of not being able to be who I am supposed to be. It is like I am looking at a mirror, and on the other side is the me I am supposed to be, but I cannot get there, because myself is in the way. I do not want to be here anymore, God. I am ready to be with You. I am ready to be like a bright star. God, I am ready to be like what Yoda said in The Empire Strikes Back. I am ready to be a luminous being. I am ready to be free.

I have been captured for a long time.

But you have set me free.

Today I am free.

Izzy will be free too. You told me to tell Izzy to escape, but I did not want to do this. I did not want to do this because that meant I had to tell her I knew things I was not supposed to know. I told You I did not want to tell her, but You said I had to tell her, so I did this, and I told her. You told me this in my heart, God. This was a good feeling. When it is a good feeling that is always You. I told her when we all got on the bus to go to the movie theater.

This is what happened.

God, we were all on the bus. The man James who owns the old movie theater invited everyone at Morning Home to his movie theater to show us a movie. So he got a bus for us to go to the theater. I could walk today and did not need the wheelchair because I think You gave me power today because it is my last day on Earth. I sat with Izzy. Ernie and Ira sat behind me. I waited until we got close to the theater because I did not want to tell Izzy, but the bus was stopping and so that is when I told her.

I said, Izzy, it is time to escape.

She made a weird face. I think she did not know what to say so she did not say anything. And I said, God told me to tell you, it is time to escape and leave. She still did not say anything. Then I said, I read your book that you told me not to read, so I know about your money. She made another weird face, and I do not think she was happy about it, but that is life. And then I said, God gave you money to do good things with, Izzy. Now you have to go to your secret bank and get it so you can use it and buy Morning Home and take care of everyone. Then she did not talk and her mouth was open wide. And she tried to say words but she did not and I told her that she has to leave right now before they see.

She said, I can't believe this.

I said, Izzy, Please do not be mad at me.

She said, I'm not mad. It's not that, not at all. It's just that I was praying, just now, right now, in my head, and I asked God for a sign.

I said, This is a normal thing, Izzy, because God always answers.

Her eyes got watery. She was crying. I did not know what to do so I gave her a hug and her face was warm. But then people were getting off the bus.

She said, When do I go, Todd?

I said, You have to go now. And when you come back, please do not forget to take care of Ernie and Ira because they will need you.

She said, I'm going to come back for you, I'm coming back for all of you.

Then Izzy gave me a hug again. It was our last hug ever. I did not tell her today was going to be my last day. All I said was, Izzy, I love you, you have been my best friend my entire whole life. She was crying even more now.

I said, I will miss you.

She told me not to worry. She told me to give her one day, but I did not have a day. I did not say this to her. She told me that she was coming back for me and Ernie and Ira and that life is going to be good from now on, and she said she would explain everything when she got back. She looked around to make sure nobody was looking, then she got off the bus and ran and ran and ran and she was free. I watched her go away until I could not see her anymore.

Then everyone went into the theater but nobody saw me. I was outside the theater alone. I walked the other way. My home with Emily was not far away.

Home is where I went.

Then I was at my home where I once lived in with Emily. I do not know how I got there. This is not something I remember. The only thing I remember is I walked away from the theater. Then I was there in front of the home where I once lived in with Emily. Then I went inside this home I once lived in with Emily.

But Emily was not there.

I went inside because You said so. You wanted me to tell Emily she did a good job. I did not want to go, but I did go, and I think that is why I do not remember how I got to my home with Emily because maybe if I knew I would not have gone. Maybe You picked me up and brought me here. I do not know. But she is not here. This is a good thing because I did not want to see Emily, even though I did. I did not want to see Emily because it was going to be too sad. I did not want to say goodbye. I did not want to see her cry. I did not want to cry either. This is why I did not want to go, but I got here anyway.

I was all alone. Then I did something I should not have done. I went into her room. I got her book that I should not read. And then I read her book that I should not read. I did this because I need to know her. When I was Body Seven and smart I knew Emily. But then I did not know her. That is why I read it.

But I knew it would hurt.

And it did hurt.

It hurt bad.

I only read one part, Part Seven. It is one of the last parts, but it is not the last last part. Emily made it like all the rest with pictures. Emily is a good drawerer. She drew many pictures like a cool comic book. Some of the things that happened in her comic book I remember. But then some of the things that happened in her comic book I do not remember. The beginning part I do not remember. That part is short. At the beginning there were pictures and it showed Emily coming home and she got the mail. In the mailbox was an envelope. One of the envelopes said it was from the New York Academy of Art. Then the pictures showed Emily running into her room and she opened the envelope. And in the envelope was a letter and the letter said Emily was accepted to the New York Academy of Art. The picture she drew showed her happy. Then it showed her crying and crying and crying. Then she was mad. Then she went into the backyard and she lit the paper on fire. Then the picture showed me a part I remember. It showed me coming outside and standing near the door, and I said to her, Emily, why are you playing with fire? Then in the comic book, Emily looked at me and she did not say anything, but she did a drawing and in the drawing it showed her thinking. In her thoughts she said that she hated me because she could not do what she wanted to do and that she had to be a nobody and do nothing and suck at life. God, that is what she wrote. But then the next drawing showed me and what I said. And in that drawing I said, Emily, why are you mad? Because I knew she was mad and this I remember. And the next drawing was another thought in the picture. And in the thought she wrote that she loved me too, and she said these words, God. She said in the thought drawing, I will give up my dream and I will not hold it against you because it's not your fault. You're just a child. And I'll never let you think it's your fault. I will not hate you. I'm going to love you.

I do not remember this part, God.

I sort of remember. I did not remember it this way. I did not remember that part because I am not inside her brain. But I do remember it because I could feel it. I remember that day because I remember that Emily was so mad at me. But I also remember I did not know why. And then I remember she changed that day and she was not mad at me at all. This is because Emily was kind to me and took care of me when she could have had a good life. She is good. This is a truth I know now. Another truth is that I have ruined her life. I am sorry. Emily did not live her life because I hurt her bad.

I hurt everyone, God.

Many people died because of me.

I died because of me.

I remember. I can not forget even though I want to. God, You know what it is but now I have to say it. It is time for me to do number four on my list.

It is time for me to forgive myself.

Thirty-One

THE CONFESSION OF TODD

God, please forgive me.

 I am sorry for my sins and I ask for forgiveness. Here is what I did. I hurt many people. I do not remember much, but I remember this. I remember what I did and it was bad. I remember the day too. That is because it was the day when I was Body Seven and I was smart, and did a bad thing and died.

 I was with my dad and it was a Sunday and it was after church on that one day when I gave my life to Jesus Christ. I wanted to watch cartoons but today I did not because my dad had to go to the grocery store. So we went to the store. And I did not want to go to the store because I always watch cartoons on Sunday that I recorded on Saturday so I could watch them twice. Also my dad was a policeman and today he did not have to work and he said he wanted to spend quality time with me, but I did not. I did not want to go, but my dad said he would buy me a comic book if I came with him, so I said yes. So we went. Then my dad was in the store and I was in the car. And I was waiting and waiting and waiting.

 Then I saw his police gun.

 The gun was in the glove box.

 And the gun looked cool.

 So I held the gun. And then my dad came out of the grocery store and I saw him walking to the car, and I got scared because I knew he would be mad if he saw me with the gun because he told me to never never never go near it. But I could not put it back in time, so I hid the gun under the seat.

Then my dad said, Here's some cash, go get whatever comic you want.

And I told him okay. He said he was going to rent us a movie and I said Star Wars and he said okay. Then I walked in the comic book store. I remember the comic book shop because it was three thirty-two West Market Street and it was across from the jewelry shop. I looked around for a comic for a long while, but I could not decide because I was thinking about how I hid the gun. I was scared that my dad would be mad. Then I got a comic book that I did not care about and do not remember because I did not care, and I walked back outside.

Then I heard many cracks.

It was like thunder.

They went CRACK CRACK CRACK.

And the person next to me fell over and he had blood all over his face and he was dead. Then I saw a person with a gun and he was shooting other people on the street. Then my dad yelled to me and told me to run and I heard him yell at me and he said my name and to run run run so then I ran and I was afraid and I did not know where I was running to but I ran and I ran and I ran and I was on a bridge and I kept running and running and I did not know where my dad was or why my dad was not with me and I remembered it was because he was a good policeman and he was going to stop the bad guy.

But I remembered I hid the gun.

I stopped running and I turned and ran back to my dad. I ran because I had to tell my dad that I hid the gun so he could kill the bad guy and also I wanted to tell him I love him because he is my dad. And then I heard more big cracks again somewhere that was not near me and I think one of the cracks is when my dad got shot and died. And then I heard a screech. And then I turned to the screech and a car was coming from behind me and the car was close and it was like a movie, God, it was like slow time, and I saw the face of the person driving and that face was Jacob. Then I do not remember anything.

This is how I became dumb.

I am happy to tell the truth.

Now I am forgiven.

Thirty-Two

NUMBER THREE THIRTY-THREE WEST MARKET STREET

God, I forgot again.

I skipped number three on my list. I needed to tell Emily she did a good job. But I was in our old home and she was not. I did not know what to do and then the phone rang so I answered it. And the person on the phone was a woman.

She said, Hello, to whom am I speaking?

I said, My name is Todd.

She said, Todd, is Emily there?

I said, No.

She said, Will you see her soon?

I said, I hope so.

She said, Well, we're looking forward to seeing her and Dr. Hemming at four-thirty to look at rings. We just wanted to confirm the appointment.

I said, Okay.

She said, So I guess we'll see them soon.

I said, You will see Emily?

She said, Yes, that is correct.

I said, Where will you see her?

She said, Here.

I said, Where?

She said, Number three thirty-three West Market Street. Right across the street from the comic book shop.

I said, Oh I know where that is.

Then I said okay bye and hung up the phone. And then I knew I had to go to three thirty-three West Market Street near the comic book shop. But my head was getting swirly and I was afraid I would not make it. So I wrote a note. This is that note that I have written, God.

Dear Emily,

I love you a lot. And now I know what you did for me even though I did not know before. I know this because I read your book and I am sorry but also I am not that sorry because I wanted to know you. You are the best sister in the entire whole world. I have prayed for you. You did a good job. This is a truth. You will have a good life now. I am coming to see you at the ring store. If I do not see you, I have wrote a note. This is the note. If I do not see you, I will miss you. But I will see you again in Heaven and I will be with mom and dad. This is a truth.

- Also this note is from Todd

Then I left the home where Emily and me once lived. I walked for a long while. I walked all over Morning and that is because I forgot where I was going. But then I remembered where I was going, and when I remembered is when I saw the ring store. I was already there. I think You picked me up and dropped me off again. I was at the corner of the street and it was at the end of the block. I saw Emily and Doctor Hemming walk inside but they did not see me. I was going to say goodbye to them. But I was afraid. I was afraid because I knew they would ask me questions. They would not understand that I am going to die today. So I did not go in right then. I just waited. While I was waiting, a truck parked next to me and it was towing something. And the thing it was towing was in a big box with bars. Then the owner got out of the truck and walked away. I went to the big box and a face stuck out through bars, and it was the face of a horse.

It was a white horse.

The horse licked me.

I knew who it was.

I said, Hello, Thunder Son.

The horse licked me again. I did not know how Thunder Son got here, but I remembered that Thunder Son can ride so fast it can travel through time and maybe other things too. I told Thunder Son I was glad he was here. And my face was hot and my eyes were watery. And I did not know I was crying but I suppose I was crying so then I was crying. And I said to Thunder Son, I did not know I was crying but I suppose I am crying so then I am crying. I think this is because I needed a friend, and God, You brought me Thunder Son. I told Thunder Son I did not know what I was supposed to do. That is because I was still afraid to go inside the store and talk to Emily and Doctor Hemming and say goodbye.

But then I understood what I had to do.

That is because I saw Jacob.

Jacob was in a hurt.

This was a bad hurt. Sometimes when people are in a hurt, they do things to hurt other people. I think that was what Jacob was doing. Because he had a gun. I think he was on drugs again. He looked weird. He had dark eyes.

I said, Jacob, why are you here?

He said, Is Emily in there?

I said, I do not know.

Then I said, Jacob, Why do you have a gun?

He said, Did you tell Emily it was me?

I did not know what he meant, but then I did know what he meant because I remembered. Jacob wanted to know if I told her that he ran me over and made me dumb and is the reason Emily had to take care of me. But I forgave Jacob and I never told anyone anything except You, God.

He said, She won't talk to me because she knows, and you told her.

I said, Nobody knows, Jacob.

He said, Then why won't she talk to me?

I said, It is because you suck.

But I felt bad for saying that, but also I did not.

He said, You remember what happened that day, don't you.

I said, I forgive you, Jacob.

Then he tried to go past me. I did not let him, God. He had a gun and I do not know what he was going to do but I knew he was not going to do anything good and I promised I would not let him hurt Emily. So I got in front of him and I pushed him hard and then he hit me with the gun. Then I pushed him again and he fell over on his back and he pointed the gun at me.

Then there was a crack.

It was loud like thunder.

And I had a bad hurt in my stomach.

I heard someone scream and his face looked afraid. Then he dropped the gun and got up and he ran away. I heard someone yell to call the police. And I sat down because I was in a hurt and I looked at my stomach and it was all red and slimy. I was in a big hurt. I just wanted to go to sleep. I was tired.

Then there was a bashing.

And a smashing.

Then a crashing.

Then I saw the face of Thunder Son. He licked me. I think he saw me get hurt and he broke out of his box. He bent down low. And he put his face near mine. I think he wanted me to get on his back. It hurt me a lot but I stood up and then I got on Thunder Son. Someone was yelling for me to lay down until the ambulance came, but I did not want to do that.

Then I rode away.

I did not have to do much. I was tired so I hugged Thunder Son my horse and Thunder Son walked away. I liked this, God. I could hear his feet clop clop clopping on the street. And the sun was in front of us going down over the hills. It was like in the movies when the cowboy rides to the sunset. I held my horse. I was tired and I told Thunder Son I was going to sleep but only for a second. So I closed my eyes.

And I went to sleep.

Thirty-Three

THAT
IS
LIFE

I opened my eyes.

God, I knew You were watching out for me, because I slept for a little and I know that because when I opened my eyes, me and Thunder Son were at the cornfield. This is the place I always go when I get lost and I need to go home. I knew where I was, but this was different because I did not know how to get home. Thunder Son bent down again and I knew I was supposed to get off, so I got off my horse and said, Thank you, Thunder Son.

I sat down. I got my book out and opened it. I wanted to write what happened but my hand shook and blood was on me and also I could not see good. I heard footsteps. Someone was in front of me. I could not see Him good, but He was shiny and He was You, Jesus. You said it was time for me to come home. I said, Home Home or Truth Home? You said, Truth Home. I said okay but I need to finish my book so Emily knows what happened, but my hand is shaky, also I am bleeding. You said, Go ahead and finish your book. Then I could write good again and it was fine. So I finished my book and I said everything that happened, and I wrote my last words which are next so Emily will know and not be sad.

You helped me stand. The sun was setting at the end of the cornfield. It was a bright Truth Light. I said, I am hoping now, hoping is my favorite thing, that is why I always hope with You. You held my hand. I said, It was a good life. You smiled back at me, and we walked toward the Bright Truth Light together.

I said, This is a good feeling.

THE END.

Made in the USA
Columbia, SC
23 October 2024